Sweet 16 to Life

Also by Kimberly Reid

Creeping With the Enemy

My Own Worst Frenemy

No Place Safe

Published by Kensington Publishing Corporation

Sweet 16 to Life

A LANGDON PREP NOVEL

KIMBERLY REID

Dafina KTeen Books
KENSINGTON PUBLISHING CORP.
http://www.kensingtonbooks.com

DAFINA KTEEN BOOKS are published by

Kensington Publishing Corp.
119 West 40th Street
New York, NY 10018

All Kensington titles, imprints, and distributed lines are available at special quantity discounts for bulk purchases for sales promotion, premiums, fundraising, educational, or institutional use.

Special book excerpts or customized printings can also be created to fit specific needs. For details, write or phone the office of the Kensington Special Sales Manager: Attn.: Special Sales Department. Kensington Publishing Corp., 119 West 40th Street, New York, NY 10018. Phone: 1-800-221-2647.

K logo Reg. US Pat. & TM Off.
Sunburst logo Reg. US Pat. & TM Off.

ISBN-13: 978-0-7582-6742-9
ISBN-10: 0-7582-6742-8

First Printing: February 2013

10 9 8 7 6 5 4 3 2 1

Printed in the United States of America

ACKNOWLEDGMENTS

I am always grateful to my readers for going on this ride with me, but there are a few who deserve a special shout-out because they named some of the characters in this book. To Candace M. Chatman, Rachael McCollum, Eva and Cher—thanks for being part of this story.

I'm forever appreciative to everyone at Kensington Publishing for taking a chance on me and my stories.

My literary agent, Kristin Nelson—thank you for being my MJ and always having my back, no matter what.

Chapter 1

I promise. That's the last thing I said to my mother before she left this morning to relieve the detectives working the graveyard shift of a 24-7 stakeout, right after I listed for the third time everything I'd promised to do:

1. Stay out of trouble. (I didn't plead my case that trouble finds me, not the other way around.)
2. Stop playing amateur detective. (I didn't point out how, for an amateur, I'd solved more big cases than she had in the last couple of months.)
3. Focus on school and make the most of the opportunity Langdon Preparatory School has given me. (I didn't blame her for the aforementioned trouble, which mostly happened because she made me go to Langdon in the first place.)
4. Choose my friends more carefully. (I didn't remind my mom that Bethanie couldn't help it if her father was a crook or that MJ might be an ex-con, but she's saved my butt a few times now.)
5. Stay out of grown folks' business.

I plan to keep all of these promises except number five; I was crossing my fingers behind my back on that one, which is why I didn't complain about the first four. Lana—which is what I call my mother instead of mom (it's an undercover cop thing)—had been hiding something from me for a while now, and a couple of weeks ago she finally admitted the big secret is my father. I prefer to think of him as my sperm donor since that's the first, last, and only thing he has ever brought to the party. He disappeared the minute Lana told him I was on the way. Sixteen years later, he started calling Lana, and she held out on me about it, pretending he was an annoying bill collector. When it became obvious her threats weren't going to stop the calls, she promised to tell me everything, but so far, the only thing she's copped to is his identity. Then she got all cryptic about how he's bad news and we don't want him in our lives.

I want to know what's so sinister about my—well, let's call him SD for short because the long version is a little too gross to think about more than once. It must be serious because he has my mother slightly unhinged and almost nothing has that effect on her. Lana works undercover in the vice division where half the job is being unflappable. She can't flinch when a pimp she's investigating threatens her. If some junkie in a crack house she's pretending to live in jumps bad on her because she's claimed his corner of the city-condemned house, Lana has to jump bad right back. She's a third-degree black belt in karate and leaves the house for work strapped, not once, but three times if you include her baton.

So when something has my mother looking over her shoulder, avoiding phone calls at the house, and worse, evading my questions, something is seriously wrong. It was better when I suspected some bad guy she put away years ago was out of jail and making threats. Now that I know it's my SD making Lana this way, it's totally my business and I'm going to figure out what his story is.

Yeah, I'm going to fit that investigation somewhere between getting my grades in shape before finals; wishing my friend Bethanie wasn't in witness protection, leaving me to deal with that viper pit of a school on my own; and pretending Marco Ruiz, my former quasi-boyfriend, doesn't break my heart every time I catch a glimpse of him at school, which is all the time and everywhere. Oh yeah, I also need to plan my birthday party. My life has become a total wreck since I started my junior year at Langdon Prep, but no matter what happens between now and my birthday, I will be celebrating my sweet sixteen in style.

I'm about to head back to bed when I think I smell smoke. I check the kitchen, but the stove is off and the coffee maker is cold. I unplug the toaster, just in case. Still smell it. There's no way Lana would have curled her hair just to sit in a surveillance van with her partner all day—even though he is hella cute and she really should make a little more effort—but I check her bathroom for a hot curling iron anyway. Nope, it's cold, too. Then I realize the smell can't be from coming from inside because Lana has a smoke detector in every room of our house.

I follow the smell to the kitchen again and notice the window isn't completely closed. I'd cracked it open to air out the kitchen last night when I burned a pizza. The smoke is outside somewhere. It's November and definitely fireplace weather, but not before eight o'clock on Sunday morning—people are either still asleep or just starting their coffee brewing. When I step out on the back porch, the smell of burning wood mixed with paint, plastic, and rubber hits me. Someone's house is on fire. Since I've made the mistake before of calling the fire department when it was just a neighbor's barbecue, I lean over the porch railing and look left, then right. That's when I see the smoke coming from the house two doors down. I grab the fire extinguisher from the kitchen pantry and call 911 from the cordless phone as I run down the street toward MJ's place.

Chapter 2

"9-1-1. What's your emergency?"

"My name is Chantal Evans. I'm reporting a fire at my neighbor's house. 698 Aurora Avenue in Denver Heights."

By the time I reach the house, the 911 dispatcher has confirmed MJ's address and has told me a truck is on the way. She tries to keep me on the phone by asking questions about me, my location, my phone number—probably because I told her I was going to the house to make sure everyone was awake and out of there—but I hang up on her. I also ignore her attempts to call me back, but not because I'm rude. For one thing, I'm not brave enough to go into a burning house so she doesn't have to worry about that. But I also need the phone to call MJ. It's definitely too early for MJ to be awake, and even her mostly God-fearing, church-going grandmother may not be up yet.

While I wait for someone to answer, I run around to the backyard to see how bad the fire is. It's still contained to the porch from what I can tell, but it's starting to snake up the porch wall, which it shares with the kitchen. Damn—my call goes to voice mail. I run around front to bang on the door, forgetting Big Mama has *rejas* on every door and window of the house, so all I can do is ring the bell. No one comes.

This whole time I've been carrying the fire extinguisher and somehow forgot I had it. The fire is too big for it to be any use, but it should make a ton of noise if I bang it against the metal bars on the front door. After about thirty seconds of banging the extinguisher against the bars, then dragging it across them, I haven't managed to awaken anyone inside the house. A weird thing to worry about at a time like this, but I check the street behind me to see if I've woken up half the neighborhood yet and I'm surprised to find only one person. There's a dude I've never seen before standing across the street in front of Ada Crawford's place. At least I'm pretty sure I've never seen him around, but there isn't much to go on as far as trying to recognize him, since he's wearing sunglasses and a jacket that must be two sizes too big for him because the hoodie covers most of his face. But I can see that he's smiling, and it sends a chill through me.

I go back to ringing the doorbell, feeling completely helpless. It's been about three minutes since I hung up with 911, and thanks to having a cop for a mother, I know the response time for the nearest firehouse is about four minutes from the time the call is dispatched. They shouldn't be late at this time of day, but what if they are? If I'm wrong and the fire is inside the house, there's been enough time for smoke inhalation to make a sleeping person inside pass out. I'm trying to decide whether I should slip something through the *rejas* to break a window and call for MJ and her grandmother. Since it's November and Big Mama likes to keep her house like an oven, I know there isn't a window open anywhere. If the fire has moved into the house and I break a window open, that's only going to accelerate the fire's movement from the back of the house to the front. But what do I do? They must be inside—where else would they be this time of day?

That's when I hear the sirens; they are close. In Denver Heights, sirens are like crickets to people in the suburbs—the sound is always there in the background so you tune them out. But I've been listening for them today, praying they live up to their four-minute response time. Now I don't have to make a decision about whether to break the window because the fire trucks are on Center Street, less than a quarter mile away. Now I hear them turning onto Aurora Ave. I'm still ringing the doorbell and calling MJ's phone for the umpteenth time when two trucks stop in front of the house.

The first man off the truck runs ups to me while the others begin their work.

"Did you call this in?"

"Yes, sir. Looks like it started around back on the porch," I say.

"Anyone in there?" he asks me while he waves the men around back.

"It's so early, they must be, even though they don't answer the phone or the doorbell. That's their car parked out front."

"How many?"

"Two. Their bedrooms are on that side," I tell him, pointing out the location. "Probably still asleep. I don't hear any smoke detectors, so maybe the fire hasn't moved inside."

"Or they don't have any. Move over there now," he says, waving. I go in the direction I think he waved. I'm not sure.

It's starting to sink in that the fire may be worse than I thought and MJ and Big Mama are in there, already passed out from lack of oxygen, and every entryway to the house is covered with iron bars. I feel kind of numb—this is all so surreal—but I move out of the path of firefighters and hoses. People are starting to come out of their homes. The strange dude is still standing in Ada's yard, but he's no longer smiling. Now he looks agitated as he stares in the direction of MJ's house, shifting his weight from one foot to another, jiggling his hands inside the pockets of his jacket. He's still wearing dark glasses even though the morning isn't bright at all, and I can only assume he's watching the firefighters work.

Just then, I spot MJ near the end of the block, coming

from Center Street. First she's walking; then she starts to jog and then breaks into a full-out run. I meet her one house away so I can try to stop her from trying to get inside. How I expect to stop a girl who has seven inches and seventy pounds on me, I don't know.

"MJ! You're okay."

"Yeah, I was at the bodega. What the hell . . . ?"

"What about Big Mama? They're prying the *rejas* off now so they can get inside."

"No, she ain't in there. She left last night on a church mission to Grand Junction. No one's in there," MJ says, although it sounds more like a question than a statement.

"Are you sure? We need to tell the firefighters."

"Yeah, I'm sure. Who else would be in there?" she asks, looking over the growing crowd. "They're going to ruin the door. I need to give them the house key."

MJ runs up to the nearest firefighter who looks the least engaged with putting out the fire. I scan the crowd, too. The dude in the hoodie is gone, but my friends Tasha and Michelle are standing in the spot he was standing just sixty seconds ago. Tasha waves at me; I wave back. Maybe I was crazy and there was never a guy in a jacket.

Then I spot him, or at least I think it's the guy because I can only see the back of him. He's walking up Aurora Ave toward Center Street, and I notice he has an odd gait. His jacket was solid brown when I saw him from the front. Now I see the back is printed in white, some kind of elaborate scroll or vector design. In the middle of the artwork are large numbers, maybe *04*, written in an Old English kind of font. I've never seen a sports jersey where the numbers were so elaborate. And I don't know much about sports, but I've been a groupie at enough of Marco's football games to know they don't use the zero in front of a number. If it's a single digit number, they just use that digit—no zero. He's getting too far away for me to see it clearly, but it's enough of a description to be helpful to the cops.

I look around for MJ so we can follow him. That's something I'd never have the nerve to do, but with MJ—former gang girl, ex-con, and still scary—I'm fearless. But by the time I turn around to make sure the guy is still walking down The Ave, he isn't. He has disappeared.

Chapter 3

MJ is still talking to the firefighter, though it looks more like she's yelling at him. She is the most chill person I know besides Lana. As much as they dislike each other, they have a lot in common, like always being cool and under control. I walk up to them and hear MJ ranting about the basement.

"Our first concern is making sure no one is inside the house, then we can check structural damage," the firefighter is saying.

I'm wondering why he even has to have this conversation when the fire *is still burning.* I think MJ has lost it.

"I told you ain't nobody in there. You need to stop the fire," MJ says, as if a man with the job title of *firefighter* doesn't know that. "It can't reach the basement."

"MJ, come on and let them do their work," I say, but she shakes my hand off her arm.

The fireman looks relieved to see someone sane trying to reason with the crazy girl. "You'd better get your friend out of my face or I'll call the police and have her arrested for obstruction," he warns.

Those are the magic words for MJ in just about any situation. MJ hates cops and will avoid having to deal with them even when she's freaked by the possibility of her house burning down—or her basement, which has suddenly become so important to her. She even apologizes, or at least gives her version of an apology.

"All that ain't necessary," she says. "I'll just wait over here."

MJ comes with me to stand in Mrs. Jenkins's yard. Mrs. Jenkins lives in the house between us and she's usually fussy about her yard. She'll yell at me if I cross it to get to MJ's place instead of using the sidewalk, and woe to anyone who lets their dog use it for a bathroom, especially if they don't clean up after. Mrs. Jenkins will spy from her living room window all day long to figure out who did it and call the cops since that's against the law. That old lady is no joke. I'm kind of surprised she never had me arrested for trespassing. But Mrs. Jenkins is mellow about us standing in her yard even though she's right there on her porch and she can see us clear as day. Either she's finally showing some sympathy for MJ, or she's afraid of Big Mama. Well, most folks are afraid of Big Mama. And MJ, for that matter.

"MJ, what's all that grief you were giving the fireman?"

"What grief? I wasn't giving no grief. I'm just worried about Big Mama's house, that's all."

"You only seemed worried about the basement."

MJ cuts her eyes at me, then goes back to watching the firemen. I don't say anything for a minute, until one of the firefighters yells to the man MJ and I had been talking to that it's contained and under control. MJ looks a little relieved, so I figure it's a good time to tell her about Hoodie Dude.

"Maybe we should let that fireman call the police, anyway," I say, and MJ looks at me like I just suggested we kick puppies.

"Not for you. For whoever started this fire."

"I know your mom is one and everything, but you still have way too much love for the Five-O, always trying to get them involved. It was probably Big Mama's space heater. It's ancient and the cord on it is all worn out."

"She keeps the central heat at eighty degrees in the winter. Why does she need a space heater?"

"Old people get chills even when it's warm. Ain't nobody started this fire, Chanti."

"When I came down here to wake y'all up, I saw this strange dude standing across the street just watching the house."

"Strange how?"

"Strange because I'd never seen him before."

"Despite you being in everybody's business twenty-four/seven, there may be a few people on this block you don't know."

"Like who?" I ask, because we both know that isn't true.

"So he was staring at the house. Half the neighborhood is out here staring at it. People are weird that way. They like to watch fire for some reason."

"Nope. You couldn't see the fire at that point. The only reason I knew your house was on fire and called 911 was—"

"You called?"

"Yeah, and only because I went out on my back porch and could see smoke coming from the back of your house, but the wind's direction made it trail away behind your house, not up above it. A minute later, I was banging on your front door and I know for a fact there was no way anyone could know about that fire from standing in the front of the house."

"Maybe dude smelled smoke."

"Maybe, but why stare at a particular house when you don't know where the smell is coming from? Most people would look up and down the street, trying to figure out which house it is. He already knew."

MJ turns away from watching the firefighters to look at me for the first time since I told her about the fire-watcher. She gives me a good hard stare, the kind that has probably made more than a few people pee their pants, but since she's my friend, I'm not so much terrified as concerned. Okay, maybe I'm a little scared.

"Leave it alone, Chanti."

Her voice is so cold that anyone else would definitely leave it alone. But I'm not anyone else. I'm her friend. And as Lana says, I just cannot leave well enough alone even when I know that's probably the best course of action.

"Look, Chanti, there is no way we're calling the cops. Big Mama's stuff is in there."

"What stuff?" I ask, thinking I might learn what was in the basement that was so important.

"You *know*," MJ says, emphasis on the word *know*.

"I'm pretty sure I don't."

She looks at me like I might be the dumbest person on the planet. Oh, right . . . her grandmother's Numbers operation, an illegal gambling game. Big Mama has been running that pretty much since we moved here, long before Lana became a cop. Lana turns a blind eye to it and acts like she doesn't know. Just like she pretends not to know Ada Crawford is a call girl. Lana says they're small fry. Living right under our noses while they operate their business gives her opportunities. She won't tell me more than that, but I always figured she meant more opportunity to catch the bigger fry.

Plus, there's the deal I made with MJ when she learned Lana was an undercover cop—if she kept her cover, Lana would never bust Big Mama. Lana doesn't know about this arrangement, but I always figured as long as Lana was holding out for the big fry, I could delay having that conversation. But I often imagine the day Lana finally busts all the criminals on our street and, in my head, it always looks like something from a Matt Damon or Angelina Jolie movie.

"There's *stuff*? I always thought it just involved old grocery store receipts and cocktail napkins with numbers written on the back of them, the stock pages of the newspaper, and a couple of phone calls made to *certain people*," I say, stressing the *certain people* part.

"Believe me, there's stuff. Incriminating stuff."

"Well, I don't want to get Big Mama arrested. Maybe once they clear you to go inside, you can get rid of all the evidence and then call the cops."

"Nobody's calling the cops, including you."

"But this guy could be dangerous, MJ. Houses are like potato chips to an arsonist—they can't torch just one. Especially after he's seen how easily these old houses light up."

"I told you—this wasn't arson."

"And not only was he staring at the house," I say, ignoring her protest, "I'm pretty sure he was smiling."

MJ gives me a look that's scarier than the first, if it's even possible.

"Not like that, MJ. He was the opposite of that. You are definitely not smiling."

"'Cause there ain't nothing funny about this."

"Exactly my point. Why would he be smiling about something as serious as a fire? We aren't smiling. Nobody on this street is smiling," I say, looking around the crowd, mostly as an excuse not to look at MJ, who I'm sure is thinking of ways to kill me, or at least to shut me up.

"Would you just listen to me when I tell you to leave it alone? And this is the last time I'm telling you to *leave it alone*."

"But MJ . . ."

"There ain't no arsonist unless you consider me an arsonist."

"What?"

"You said the fire was in the back of the house, right?"

"Yeah. So?"

"So I think maybe I started the fire."

Chapter 4

Right after MJ drops that bomb, she leaves to find the fireman who was threatening to arrest her. She'd rather talk to him than be interrogated by me, because that's exactly what I plan to do the minute the trucks leave and everyone on the street goes back to their beds or morning coffee. Except I can't wait that long, and I know I won't get a straight story from MJ on how the fire started, anyway. So I follow her and help myself to the conversation she's having with the fireman.

"Luckily, the fire was contained to the porch and didn't damage the kitchen wall or do any structural damage," the fireman is saying when I join them.

"That means nothing inside the house got burned?" MJ asks.

"The door between the porch and kitchen got a little singed and you have some smoke damage on the walls around the door, but nothing more than that. We'll let you go in as soon as we finish our report. You'll need to air it out though. It'll probably take a few days for the smoke smell to completely clear. It might be a good idea to stay somewhere else tonight."

The fireman probably thinks MJ is relieved she won't have to find a new place to live, but I'm sure she's just worried about Big Mama's gambling supplies, which must be in the basement. Now that I think about it, seems like MJ should still be worried. Even though the fire didn't do much damage inside the house, I'm guessing whoever is making the fire report is going to walk through the house, anyway. A minute ago, MJ looked as though she was carrying the world in her arms, but now she looks like someone just took it off her hands. Maybe she figures firefighters aren't as observant to the clues of criminal activity as a cop would be.

"So can you tell us how the fire started?" I ask the fireman, making sure I avoid looking at MJ, who I'm sure is giving me the evil eye right now.

"We can't confirm anything until we get the report. Are you also an occupant of the home?"

"No, she's just a nosey neighbor," MJ says. "Chanti, don't you have somewhere to be?"

Just then, I see Lana's car coming down the street. I can take a hint—when I want to—and leave MJ and the fireman to talk. MJ calls my name and when I turn around, she nods toward Lana's car, then slowly shakes her head. It doesn't matter—I know the only reason Lana is back home is because she already knows about the fire, so it's not like it's some big secret. She probably heard 911 dispatch the call on her radio, depending on which radio band she was tuned to. Besides, MJ ought to know by now that I won't bust her to Lana, especially not when I think she's lying about starting the fire.

I reach the house as Lana is getting out of her car.

"Just as I was arriving at my stakeout location, I heard the call over the radio," Lana says, confirming my guess. "You didn't answer the phone when I called—not the landline or your cell, so I had to come check it out. Is everyone okay?"

"They're fine. No one was home. That was you calling? I thought it was the 911 dispatcher calling back and I needed the line open."

"You called in the fire?"

"Yeah. I left my cell at home and came down here while I called it in on the cordless landline. Wanted to make sure the dispatchers got the location right."

"So you remembered what I said about it being easier for dispatch when you call from a fixed location."

"Yep. Then I called MJ and Big Mama to make sure they were awake. When they didn't answer, I started banging on the doors."

"Good work. But I know you weren't trying to go inside that house," Lana says, her tone implying it was a question, not a statement, and that I'd better agree.

"Believe me, I didn't forget what you taught me about a burning structure. Which reminds me—I left our fire extinguisher down there."

"You got close enough to the fire to use an extinguisher?"

"No, but I also remember what you taught me about being prepared. I was just talking to the fireman when you got here. He said it was confined to the back porch, no structural damage, just smoke."

Lana steps back, hands on hips, and smiles. "I guess I can get back to my stakeout since you have everything under control here."

"Uh-huh, all under control. On your way home tonight, can you pick up some Popeyes?"

"Good idea. I don't feel like cooking tonight," Lana says, opening the car door.

"Can you also pick up the fire report?"

Lana closes the car door without getting inside. I knew I wouldn't fool her by sliding that request in right behind the request for a two-piece with biscuit.

"All right, Chanti, what's up?"

"Nothing's up. I just thought it would be good to know how the fire started. What if there's an arsonist working the neighborhood? Seems like we should rule out that possibility."

"Look—you did a great job calling 911 and making sure no one was inside. One day you're going to make an excellent cop—"

"I don't want to be cop," I say, which is mostly true, though my history would probably indicate otherwise. I love solving crimes, but I'm too chicken to ever be a cop.

"Did the fireman say something to indicate he suspects arson?"

What to do? I could lie and tell her yes, that's exactly what he said. But there's a fifty-fifty chance she'd know I was lying since that's what the Denver Police Department pays her to do all day. Or I could be truthful and say the fireman didn't know yet, which would mean I'd never get to see that report. If there's no immediate threat, Lana will forget all about it and go back to the million other things she's juggling. Since MJ is lying about starting that fire—a mystery in itself—I know *she'll* never let me see the report. So I choose to ignore Lana's question and take another tack.

"When I got to MJ's house, I noticed this guy I've never seen before standing across the street in Ada Crawford's yard."

"Well, last night *was* Saturday night—one of Ada's busiest. There's nothing suspect about that."

That's just like Lana, being a cop and pointing out something I hadn't thought of. But I am undeterred.

"So maybe he was a client, but why was he staring at MJ's house? Seems to me he'd be trying to get out of there quick since he'd just spent the night with a prostitute. Plus he didn't look like one of Ada's usual clients—too young, poorly dressed, and no car."

"He was probably watching the fire."

"Not a chance. At that point, you couldn't tell there was a fire from the front of the house. Like I told MJ, I only knew because I saw the smoke from our back porch. You couldn't see any flames, and the wind was blowing the smoke back toward the alley, not the street. The whole Ave was quiet, no one had come out of their houses until the sirens came down the street. But here's this stranger just standing there and staring at the house."

Lana doesn't speak right away and I know that I've hooked her.

"Maybe I should go down there and talk to whoever's in charge. Falcone will be pissed I'm late, but he can wait a few."

"Uh, no, you should probably get going. No need to get Falcone mad at you." Or get MJ mad at me.

"The report probably won't be complete for a few days, but I'll submit a request for it. In the meantime, you mind your own business," she says, opening the car door and getting in this time. "Oh, and in case I forget to tell you tonight, we have a new phone number."

"What? Why?"

"You never use that line, anyway. I have to get back to my stakeout," Lana says over the loud cranking engine of her ancient but reliable Hyundai.

"But what if *he* tries to call?"

"That's exactly why I had it changed."

"You can't keep running from him. Or me."

She ignores me and puts the car in gear.

"Wait—you didn't tell me the new number?"

"Call your cell from the landline to get it, but don't give it out to anyone yet, even your grandparents. Unless he bribed someone at the phone company, that's the only way he could have gotten the old one. He might persuade them to give him the new number," she yells as she backs the car out of the driveway. She's using one of my classic avoidance moves—the info-dump and run. It's usually effective, at least until it catches up with me, because the problem with that move is I only use it when I'm hiding something. Everyone knows secrets will eventually come back to bite you.

Chapter 5

I've spent the last couple of days working on my powers of forgetfulness, which is close to impossible since I remember everything. I'm trying to forget about the guy I'm sure attempted to burn down MJ's house, the fact that MJ said *she* actually started the fire, and the reality that Lana is so afraid of my SD that she's willing to change the phone number we've had forever. I'm also trying to accept the fact that Marco Ruiz and I are now *just friends*—the relationship status that isn't. Since he didn't like me playing amateur detective and his parents forbade me to date him after I almost got us killed by my neighbor-turned-gangster, I don't have much choice because I'm not willing to change me just to win him. Compromise I could do, but he wants me to be someone else altogether. It doesn't help that he recently hooked up with his ex-girlfriend, Angelique. And I mean *recently*, like the corpse of our relationship wasn't even cold yet.

At the end of the school day, I'm standing at my locker looking for my French book when I hear a male voice behind me call my name. It doesn't sound like Marco's voice; it's slightly deeper but still familiar, so I flash through several scenarios in the three seconds it takes me to turn around:

1. It's Marco, but he went hoarse calling plays during the football game on Saturday, which he won, of course. Now I need to put on my best I'm-cool-with-us-just-being-friends face while I explain how I didn't get a chance to congratulate him afterward because I was too busy counting all the ways I hate Angelique, who I watched cheer him on the whole game (instead of watching him) while I sat in the bleachers behind her and her shiny, bouncy, model-wavy ponytail.
2. It's Marco, and he must have caught a cold over the weekend and he knows I keep a mini first-aid kit in my locker—always prepared—and he's wondering if I might have some cough drops in there, and thanks for the drugs but he'd better get home now, no time to chat about how he broke my heart.
3. It's Marco, and he has a sore throat from fighting with his girlfriend and his parents all weekend and now he wants to tell me how wrong he was to dump me and how desperately he wants me back.

Since all the scenarios involve it being Marco standing behind me, I'm way disappointed to find it's Reginald Dacey and not Marco at all, but I try hard not to show it.

"Reginald, you're finally back at Langdon. I thought you were supposed to come back a few weeks ago."

"I hope that means you've been looking for me," he says, and I notice that while he isn't Marco cute, he's kinda cute, and a lotta presumptuous.

"No, I just remember you telling me that at my friend Bethanie's going-away party."

"Well, that was the plan until I met with Headmistress Smythe. She won't transfer my fall semester credits from my current school, so I'll have to start in January and still do my full senior year at Langdon."

"Which means you'll graduate a semester late. That's a bummer."

"It isn't so bad—I can run track here this spring, which will open up my scholarship chances. Besides," he says, lowering his voice just barely, "I get an extra semester to hang out with Chanti Evans. I'm just here today to talk to my advisor, but I lucked out running into you."

This is the point where I usually get totally awkward with boys—when I finally figure out they're flirting with me and that I'm expected to flirt back—or at least say something clever. But it never seems to work out like that, especially when the boy has eyes like Reginald's, a mix of brown and amber and apparently possessing mind control powers because I can't stop looking into them.

"I'm thinking maybe it wasn't so much luck," I say.

"Then what was it?"

"The teachers' offices aren't in this building. You were at Langdon for three years before Headmistress Smythe expelled you, so you can't be lost."

"You think I planned to run into you?"

"I'm just saying . . ." Wait, is this *me* throwing around the witty banter with a boy? A senior boy, no less. I'm not sure where it's coming from, but I keep on throwing it before the spell wears off. ". . . it does seem a little coincidental."

Reginald smiles. Yes, definitely cute. "I remember our conversation from that party, too. You promised to look out for me when I got back to Langdon."

You mean when I was just using you as a flirtation device to make Marco jealous?

"I do remember that, but you aren't back yet. Besides, isn't it enough that I'm the reason you're back? If I hadn't proven to Smythe it wasn't you who defaced Langdon property and that she'd expelled the wrong person, we wouldn't even be having this conversation."

I'm so good at this, it's beginning to feel like I've landed in a romantic comedy, with all my lines memorized and rehearsed. I was never this smooth with Marco.

"Good point," he says. "I guess I owe you."

"I guess you do."

"My mom told me you usually take the bus home—and where your locker is—so I thought maybe I could give you a ride since she gave me the car today."

"No fair using your mother to do reconnaissance on me," I say, pretending I'm miffed, but really I love his mom. Now that Bethanie's gone, Mildred Dacey—head custodian and my Langdon informant—is pretty much the only real friend I have here besides Marco. And since we broke up, we don't really hang out all that much except to work on our French semester project. When Madame Renault paired me up with Marco at the beginning of the semester, I wanted to hug her. Now it makes things more than a little awkward. My friend situation at Langdon is actually kind of sad. Good thing Reginald is coming back soon.

"Yeah, I know a little something about you, girl detective. I thought you'd be impressed with my recon work."

"Maybe I am—" I say, so into playing Coy Girl that I don't even notice Marco coming toward us until he's already there, walking smack into the middle of our witty repartee and completely breaking the spell, making me forget the witty thing I was about to say next.

"Hey, Chanti," Marco says, giving Reginald a hard look and then totally dismissing him by turning his back to him. "You were going to let me copy your French notes from last Thursday, since I missed that class. And I thought we were going to work on our project this week."

"Um, we never confirmed a date, right? Or did we?" I ask, my normal unsmooth self suddenly making a comeback. Without even trying, this boy can get me all kinds of flustered.

"She'll have to get that to you tomorrow, man," Reginald says, stepping around Marco to stand beside me. "We were just leaving, right, Chanti?"

"We were? Oh, that's right, Reginald is giving me a ride home."

Marco looks crushed. Maybe *crushed* is too strong a word. But he does look disappointed, just like I must have looked to Reginald a few minutes ago when I discovered he was behind me, not Marco. Does it make me a bad person to admit I'm doing a little happy dance inside?

"The French exam is tomorrow and I was hoping to study the notes tonight," Marco says, more to Reginald than to me.

"I guess I'll call you tonight, Marco. We can divvy up the work over the phone."

"And the notes? We've got an exam tomorrow."

"I'll scan them to you," I say—just before I bang my locker door shut, tell Reginald I'm ready to go, and leave Marco standing there. I'm hoping he's still in front of my locker watching us, noticing how I walk closer to Reginald than necessary, but I stay cool and don't look back. Not until we're at the school entrance anyway, and then I just have to turn around. Yes! Marco's been there the whole time—watching me walk away with another boy.

Seeing Marco apparently removed the Coy Girl spell permanently. Once Reginald and I were in his car, I couldn't think of a single cute thing to say. It wasn't the usual where I just get tongue-tied around boys unless I'm interrogating them. It was seeing Marco and remembering how much I want him—and all the reasons why I'm a little afraid to have him. Like how my friend Tasha found out he was a player when he was at his old school, which is the reason his thing with Angelique has always been on-again, off-again. It's hard to imagine about a guy as sweet as Marco, but Tasha isn't the only person I've heard it from. So how does a girl keep score with a player when she's clueless about the rules of the game? It's hopeless. And yet . . .

You know how when you were a kid and you thought you'd explode from the anticipation of waiting for Christmas morning, or a trip to the water park on the hottest day of July, or a summer vacation to Disney World? Imagine anticipating all those things at once. That's how Marco makes me feel every time I see him. When you feel like that about a guy, you might let him beat you at chess even if you're the better player or give up sleuthing for him just because he asks. Maybe you'd be like Lana and give up something more so that nine months later, you're having a kid at sixteen but then you never hear from the boy again. Well, not until sixteen years later, in Lana's case.

Nope, I promised myself I won't be that girl. I have plans that don't involve diapers and daycare. And I won't be the off-again part of his Angelique romance. Besides, unless he stops thinking of my sleuthing as The Big Bad Thing, it doesn't matter anyway. It was fun showing Marco that someone else is interested in me even if he isn't, and it was safe playing that game with Reginald because he doesn't make me feel like I'm on anticipation overdose. Still, on the ride to Denver Heights all I could think about was how I'll never have Marco. So when Reginald asked if I wanted to get something to eat, I directed him to TasteeTreets in a tone so dry he'd have gotten more play if he'd let the woman who voices the GPS directions tell him how to get there.

When he opens the door for me at TasteeTreets, I'm trying to figure out how to get back the flirting mojo I had earlier when I see a guy in a jacket sitting with his back to the door. Not just any jacket, but a hoodie with a scroll design and some letters written in an Old English font. He's wearing his hood up so I can make it out, even though the booth is hiding all but the very top of the design. I turn around to leave, running into Reginald's very muscular chest and I also notice that he smells really good. So I hate what I'm about to do but I have to.

"Look, Reginald, this was a bad idea," I say, heading out the second set of doors and into the cold November air.

"I thought you picked this place because you love their shakes, but we can go someplace else, no worries."

"No, it's not the place. It's just . . . you know the guy who wanted my French notes?" I say, deciding the truth, or mostly the truth, was as good an excuse as any to get rid of Reginald fast.

"Yeah."

"We recently broke up and I guess I'm not quite over him."

"I thought there was something going on between you two back there. Guess that explains why you were so quiet on the ride over," he says, and I'm surprised he seems disappointed. I know I helped him get back into Langdon, but is he really interested in more?

"I thought I was okay with the breakup, but then seeing him and everything . . ."

"You sure you can't stay? It's just a couple of chocolate shakes between new friends."

"I know, but it feels weird to me. I'm sorry. It's just that I'm really mixed up right now."

"Can I at least take you home?"

"No, I'll walk. It's just a block from here."

I don't want the guy in the jacket to leave before I get a chance to bump into him by accident and find out if he's the same boy from the fire.

"So you have to go, Reginald. Like, now." Rude much?

"All right, if you say so. I guess I'll see you around next semester, then," Reginald says, looking completely confused. I don't blame him after the way I was flirting with him back at school. But as much as I'd probably enjoy hanging out with him, I need to do some investigating first. So after I wave good-bye to Reginald and watch his car disappear into the Center Street traffic, I go back inside Treets.

Imagine my surprise when I see Hoodie Dude now has a dining companion joining him with a tray of food—MJ Cooper. They haven't spotted me so I turn around and go back outside where I can watch them without being seen. Sure, that can't be the only brown hoodie with white scroll-work in all of metro Denver. It's just a major coincidence that MJ's friend has the same jacket as the guy I think tried to burn down her house. I'm having a hard enough time trying to convince myself of this story, but it doesn't help when the guy stands up to dig into his jeans pocket and I can see the full back of his jacket. The day of the fire when he was halfway down the block, I thought the numbers *04* were written in an Old English font in the middle of all the scroll-work. But now I can read it clearly, and they aren't numbers. They're two letters: *DH*.

And I know what it stands for: the *Down Homes,* MJ's old gang.

Chapter 6

I'm not sure how long I stood outside the restaurant staring at MJ and my suspect having shakes and burgers like it's nothing but a thing to burn down your grandmother's house. It may have been five minutes or five seconds, but I didn't move until some rude—and apparently very hungry—girl told me to stop blocking the door and get the hell out of her way.

I want to storm in there and ask MJ if she's crazy, but that seems pretty obvious, not to mention it would tip her off that I'm on to them. But I need to talk to someone about this before I explode. It can't be Lana. She's still at work and besides, she isn't MJ's biggest fan even though the girl has saved my life a few times now, and I mean literally. She has softened up some, but for Lana, that only means she no longer wants to haul MJ off to jail every time she sees her. My mom comes from the once-a-felon-always-a-felon school of thought when it comes to ex-cons. And even though I've spent the last few months defending MJ, recent developments leave me wondering.

So I go to the only other person I trust with secrets, my best friend Tasha. We've known each other forever, and I could trust her with just about anything, even though she's Aurora Avenue's official gossip. She keeps all my stuff private;

the only major secret I've never told her is that Lana's a cop. It's best that as few people as possible know about that. The only reason MJ knows is because she found out by accident.

I walk the block from Treets to my street and get to Tasha's house just in time to catch her locking her front door.

"You're leaving?" I ask the obvious.

"Yeah, I have a shift at the theater tonight."

"I thought your dad said no working on school nights."

"Normally I don't, but someone called in sick so my manager asked me to come in."

"What excuse did you give your father?"

"I didn't need an excuse," Tasha says in a low voice and motions me to follow her down the porch steps. "The hospital cut my mom's hours twenty percent. We could use the extra money."

"Oh," I say, understanding all the secrecy. Her father is about the proudest man I know when it comes to his family and stuff like money. He'd hate it if anyone on the street knew they were having problems. She doesn't even have to ask me to keep it quiet.

"Walk me to the bus?"

I do, but I decide the last thing Tasha needs right now is me going on and on about MJ returning to a life of crime. She doesn't need to hear about other people's problems, especially not MJ's since I neglected our friendship for a while when MJ first moved onto Aurora Ave. Tasha trusts MJ even less than Lana does. So I stay mostly quiet and let her tell me about her new job at the movie theater downtown and her supervisor, whose hotness makes it easier for her to say yes to working on a school night.

"I like him a lot, but I don't think he knows I exist—I mean, in any other way than where I am on the weekly schedule."

"He *is* your boss. Even if he liked you, he'd get in all kinds of trouble if he told you so."

"Not from me," Tasha says. "I'd never tell a soul."

"Sure you wouldn't, at least not until you caught him with some other chick, then it would hit the fan. I mean, that's probably what he's thinking. He's not trying to get his company sued for sexual harassment."

"I suppose. That's a better reason for why he ignores me. Thanks."

"No problem. Any time you need a legal or criminal excuse why a guy isn't interested, I'm here for you."

"Yeah, you and your cop and lawyer shows. I guess all that TV watching is good for something."

When we get to the bus stop, Tasha still has a couple of minutes before it's due, so I wait with her. It reminds me of when we were little and hustled riders for money during summer vacation. We'd hang out in the bus shelter waiting for someone to need change for the $1.50 fare. We'd give them seventy-five cents on the dollar, because they'd rather give us a quarter than give the bus driver fifty cents. The bodega across the street would make them buy something and nothing in that place costs less than a quarter. Of course Lana never knew anything about our entrepreneurial spirit, but I always figured it was the same as what she always said about the prices at 7-Eleven—you have to pay for convenience. Besides, nearly everyone on the Ave has a hustle; ten-year-old kids are no exception. Tasha and I made a couple of bucks a day doing that, more than enough to keep us in candy for the week.

"So what's up with the boy you *still* haven't told me much about? Will he be your birthday date?"

"Marco? Good thing I didn't tell you much. That was over before it even started. He's already back with his ex, and I'll be having a dateless birthday."

"What happened?"

"You know, the usual."

"Did you borrow that answer from boy-of-the-month

Michelle? There is no usual for you. It may not have lasted long, but he was your first boyfriend."

"Look, there's your bus," I say relieved I don't have to talk about my very sad—and very brief—romantic history.

After Tasha boards, I realize I'm still stressing about seeing MJ with the possible arsonist, so I consider texting my only other good friend on the Ave to see if she wants to hang out. True, Michelle and I probably wouldn't say more than "hi" to each other if not for Tasha bringing us together, so *good friend* might be a bit strong. But she could be useful in a situation like this since she's been known to run with criminals— namely her ex-boyfriend Donnell. On the other hand, the reason he's her ex is because my detective work landed him in jail, and Michelle is still using that as a reason to barely tolerate me, even if she knows I did the right thing by getting him busted.

I'm still sitting on the bus shelter bench when I notice MJ leaving Treets with Hoodie Dude. They don't linger on the sidewalk for a minute before going their separate ways the way friends do. From what I can tell, they don't even say good-bye. MJ just jaywalks across Center Street headed for home, and Hoodie Dude walks straight toward the bus shelter. I pull out my phone, pretend to make a call, then turn my body away from the direction of his approach, like I'm trying to get as much privacy for my call as anyone could in a bus shelter. I hope he didn't get a good look at me before I realized he was coming my way, and if he did, that he won't recognize me from the day of the fire. My heart is pounding when I feel his weight land on the bench beside me.

But I guess he doesn't recognize me because when I sneak a quick peek, I see he has taken out his own phone and begun texting. I want to get out of there, but I make myself stay. Maybe he'll make a call and I'll hear him say something incriminating. After a couple of minutes, he's still texting and

I begin to feel stupid holding my end of an imaginary phone call. I'm about to leave the shelter when I notice an odd smell.

It would probably be hard for anyone who doesn't live near the corner of Aurora Avenue and Center Street to smell anything other than the grease Treets uses to deep-fry fish, dry-cleaning fluid, bus exhaust, and the sesame oil-scented smoke from Seoul BBQ. But this corner is as familiar to me as my own home and I know an out-of-place scent when I smell one, and I didn't detect this one until Hoodie Dude arrived. It's the smell of smoke, but different from the spicy grilled-meat smoke pouring out of stacks on Seoul BBQ's roof. This is the smell of wood smoke, tinged with something else I can't quite make out. Maybe bacon? I guess I'm picking up on a blend of Eau de Hoodie Dude and TasteeTreets value meal #8—the Extreme BLT.

But the smoke smell is unmistakable, and it's also strong. It's been two days since MJ's house almost burned down. I suppose Hoodie Dude could have gone camping and built a fire since then, or maybe he has a fireplace at home. But I suspect a guy who goes around in the same jacket all the time even when it stinks of smoke probably doesn't live in the kind of home that has a washer and dryer, much less a fireplace. And two-day-old smoke doesn't smell this strongly on the clothes of someone who watched a fire from across the street.

"Hey, you got the time?"

His voice startles me, but I know he doesn't really need the time from me because he was just on his phone. Maybe he did see me when he first came out of Treets and recognized me from the day of the fire. But I don't turn around when I answer, "Nope. My battery just died."

I see the bus approaching from a block away and get up to leave the shelter before Hoodie Dude does so I can pretend to board first. When the bus doors open, I dig around in my bag, mumble something about forgetting my bus pass and walk in the direction the bus came from. That way when he boards—*if* he boards—he won't be able to look back to see my face.

Chapter 7

Hoodie Dude does board the bus instead of following me, and by the time I take a left down the next block and double back toward Aurora Avenue, I'm beginning to think maybe I was just being a little paranoid. Maybe the guy really was just asking the time. After years of riding the city bus, I know by now that's one of the oldest lines guys use to start a conversation because it's a legit question when you're waiting for a bus. Still, I don't feel that great about going home to an empty house.

I figure since I don't have anyone to tell my problems to and I cancelled my impromptu date with Reginald, I should at least do right by Marco and my GPA, and start walking south toward Lexington Avenue. It's too early for him to be home from football practice yet, and I don't want to risk knocking on his door and having his parents be home since they generally hate me. He says *I'm* the reason we aren't to-gether, not them, since I chose pretending to be Nancy Drew over him. His parents don't want me with him because I'm allegedly *dangerous*. You solve a few small crimes and almost get killed twice and people typecast you. So I stand at the end of his block pretending to wait at the bus stop on the corner. Nearly an hour later, I have waved off three buses by the time

I finally see his car turn onto his street. Not a minute too soon because it's late November in Colorado and the sun is already lost behind the mountains, which means I'm probably in danger of losing a couple of toes to frostbite if I stand on this corner much longer. Or maybe give the wrong impression to the cop who's driven by a few times now.

I walk/run down the block to Marco's house, mostly walking because I swear my feet are frozen, but I still manage to reach his house before he goes inside. He doesn't see me coming because he's leaning into his trunk gathering all his football gear. When he stands up and finds me there, he's startled.

"Jesus, Chanti, why you have to sneak up on someone like that? You know that can get you hurt around here."

"Sorry," I say, handing him the cleats he dropped when I surprised him.

"What are doing you here, anyway?"

"Nice to see you, too. You were right about our French project. We really should start working on it."

"Where's that dude? I thought you were hanging out."

Oh, that. While I was waiting for Marco to get home, I was so focused on MJ going back to her criminal ways that I'd completely forgotten about Reginald and the whole I-can-get-another-boy-if-I-want project.

"No, not hanging out. He just gave me a ride home because I lost my bus pass and he had his mom's car today."

Marco closes his trunk and stops for a second to stare at me, a little longingly if you ask me.

"You look cold."

"I'm freezing. I've been waiting a while."

"Here?"

"I knew your parents wouldn't like me here and that you'd still be at practice, so I waited down on the corner until I saw your car coming."

"They also wouldn't want you to die of hypothermia. Besides, no one's home. Come in and warm up."

He leads me into their kitchen, which is more of the house than I saw when we were sort of together, since I never actually made it inside. It's nothing like I expected, which I now realize was a stereotype: Mexican rugs, a crucifix in every room, Kokopelli sand art, and paintings of sombrero and poncho-wearing farmers in the desert. Since I've seen all those things in every house I've been in that was designed in Southwestern décor—and you see a lot of that when you live in Colorado—I figured that's what would be in an actual Mexican home. But I was way wrong—everything is in sleek chrome, glass, and black leather. Well, pleather. And from what I can see, there's only one crucifix—a tiny one hanging in the kitchen next to the phone on the wall.

Marco gestures me toward the kitchen table, then takes down a mug from the cabinet.

"Hot cocoa okay?" he says, holding up a packet of Swiss Miss.

"Perfect," I say, watching him mix the powder and water before he puts the mug in the microwave. He's wearing a long sleeved T-shirt with the sleeves pushed up just enough for me to see his muscular forearms. Yep, perfect.

"That'll take a couple of minutes, just enough time to make copies in my mom's office."

"She works from home?" I ask as I take my French notebook out of my backpack.

"No, she teaches science at North Denver Heights, but teachers only do half their jobs at school. There's all the grading and stuff to do at home. I'll be back in a sec."

That's some good information—that his mother is a science teacher. I love science. Maybe one day that'll work in my favor to win hers. With Marco gone, I'm tempted to snoop around the kitchen, but I don't. Even if his on-again girl is back in the picture and I'm mega-confused about whether I'm even ready for a boyfriend, maybe by the time I finally figure it out, Marco will have remembered why he left Angelique in the first place. I'd hate to ruin my chances all because I couldn't help my nosey self. So I check out what I can from my seat at the table.

It's amazing what you can learn from a family's refrigerator door, and what I learn in two minutes is that Marco is clearly the star of the family and he isn't even an only child. His older brother is away in the military, but still . . . Marco is in every last picture, at the center of them all. My mom has a couple of me on the fridge, but they're mixed in with my grandparents, Lana's cop friends during a girls' night, her partner Falcone holding a big fish he'd just caught, and there are one or two people I don't recognize. And my photos are recent. Marco's family has pictures of him ranging from his first birthday right up to him in his Langdon Knights football uniform. I'm the first to admit he's the cutest thing ever, but somebody went overboard. There's one photo with another boy besides Marco, who I'm guessing is his brother, though he looks too young. I'm about to go in for a closer look, but just then, Marco returns with my notebook.

"Thanks," we say at the same time, to which I add, "Jinx!" and immediately feel like a dork. I bet Angelique acts like she's seventeen instead of seven, though in my defense, I'm not even sixteen yet. I'm relieved when the microwave pings and hopefully distracts him.

"I can't believe you stood out in the cold waiting for me," Marco says as he hands me the mug. Our fingers touch just for a second, but it warms me more than the cocoa will. He turns a chair backward, straddles it, and leans his arms against the back. I love the way guys do that.

"I didn't want you to flunk French because of me."

"Still, that's pretty dedicated. I mean, it's what—fifty degrees out?"

The way he says it, I'm beginning to feel less like a considerate study partner and more like a desperate ex-girlfriend. It doesn't help that I keep staring at his shoulders and how they look a little broader than I remember. Must be all the football workouts.

"What?" he asks, smiling. Oh my God, did he notice me staring? If he did, he decides to let me off the hook. "I need to send a quick text, then we can hit the books."

He keeps talking while he texts. I try hard not to stare at him even though he's looking down at his phone. I notice his hair is still the teeniest bit damp from his after-practice shower.

"I thought what's-his-name gave you a ride home."

"Reginald? He did."

"But you still have a full backpack. And you're still in your school uniform."

Dang with all the questions. He's been hanging around me too much.

"Okay, so he didn't take me home. We went to Tastee Treets, but before we made our order, I realized you and I really needed to get started on the project. I told Reginald I'd have to take a rain check and walked straight here, full backpack, uniform and all," I lie, hoping he didn't notice how I kept fidgeting as I told it, even though it's only partly a lie. I can sell a lie to just about anyone, even Lana half the time, but not so much with Marco. Maybe I did have ulterior motives for dropping by.

"Is anything else going on? You seem different than when I saw you a couple of hours ago. Did you and Reginald have a fight or something?"

"There is no me and Reginald," I say a little too quickly, especially since a couple of hours ago I was trying to show him that other boys were interested. In an attempt to look less desperate, I try to change the subject. "I saw something over the weekend that really shook me up. I guess it's still on my mind."

"What happened?"

"A friend on my street almost had her house burn down."

"Wow, that would shake me up, too."

"Everyone is okay and I called 911 early enough so there wasn't a lot of damage. But the fire wasn't the disturbing part. Before the fire trucks came, I saw a guy watching the fire. He was smiling, like he was watching a fireworks show."

"That's messed up."

"I'm saying. So I told my friend about it, and how I suspected this guy might have started it."

Marco stiffens a little, but I read his body language wrong.

"No, that wasn't the scary part, either. It was seeing my friend today at TasteeTreets with the suspected arsonist."

"Wait, is this about some case you're working on?" Marco asks. "Because I don't want to know."

"You asked if something was up, and I told you."

"Because I thought you were really upset about something, not trying to get yourself killed again."

"I thought the only reason you didn't like me playing detective was because your parents wouldn't let us be together if I did. Now we aren't together. You're with Angelique and we're just friends."

"And I thought you were here because you wanted to see me—to work on the project—not talk about some investigation. Why couldn't you tell Reginald about it? He's your friend."

"Because I saw my neighbor with the guy after Reginald left Treets, and he isn't my friend. I barely know him."

Marco goes quiet, so I ask, "Would you be . . . angry if I started hanging out with Reginald?"

"What? Hell no," he says, jumping up from the chair. "Like you said, we're just friends and I'm with Angel. You can be friends with whoever you want."

"That's why I thought I could bounce some ideas off of you before I confront my friend with all this."

He sits again, but this time he turns the chair the right way, and sits the right way, crossing his arms against his chest. This time, I read the body language correctly.

"Okay, but you can't stay long," he says.

"Will your parents be here soon?"

"No, but Angel will."

Oh, right. Angel. But I pretend it doesn't faze me and tell him the little I know so far about MJ and my suspect, including the part about MJ's unfortunate incarceration.

"Why would your friend want to burn down her grandmother's house? Does she hate her or something?"

"That's what I don't get. She loves Big Mama. I was thinking maybe an insurance scam. It's really the only thing I can think of."

"But her grandmother would have to be in on it. She's the one holding the insurance policy."

"That isn't out of the question. Big Mama has a shady side, too."

"Who are these people you hang out with? It's no wonder you're always in the middle of some trouble."

"They're good people, mostly. And it isn't *my* trouble."

"That's exactly the point I've been trying to make for the last three months."

We stare at each other a second too long before I pick up the brainstorming again.

"But she was so worried about something being damaged in the basement. MJ isn't the smartest girl on the block, but if she was in on it, she'd have enough sense to move whatever she's trying to protect before the arsonist started the fire."

"So maybe she wasn't part of it. What makes you sure this guy is an arsonist, anyway?"

"The way he was just standing there, watching the house but not helping me when he could see I was frantically trying to rescue MJ and her grandmother. The way he knew there was a fire even though you still couldn't see the smoke from the front of the house. I thought I was the first person to know there was a fire until I saw him. If he knew about it, why didn't he call it in?"

"Maybe he's just a freak who gets off on watching fires. Doesn't mean he started it."

"That would make him even more dangerous than a garden-variety arsonist. I just wish I'd gotten a good look at his face."

"How do you know the guy in TasteeTreets was the same guy if you didn't get a good look at him?"

"He was wearing the same hoodie."

"Lots of guys wear hoodies, Chanti."

"Not hoodies that reek of smoke."

"You got close enough to sniff the dude?" Marco asks.

It makes me laugh because I get a visual of what he must be imagining—me going up to the guy and getting my basset hound on.

When I compose myself, I say, "No, I didn't have to sniff him, exactly. He sat down next to me at the bus stop, a foot away, and I could still smell the smoke on him."

"Are you crazy, Chanti? Let's say you're not paranoid and the guy really is an arsonist. What part of stalking a firestarter do you think is a good idea?"

"I didn't stalk him. I was already at the bus stop. *He* joined me."

"Okay, so the guy smelled like a fireplace. That and a hoodie still aren't enough to make him an arsonist."

"Not when the hoodie has the letters *DH* on the back, which are, coincidentally enough, the initials of MJ's old gang."

"And Elvis is still alive and the government is hiding aliens in Roswell." He gets up from the table again, and this time slides his chair under, like he's done with the conversation.

It takes me a second to realize he's making fun of me.

"How can you say I'm one of those crazy conspiracy theorists? You were there when I busted that very real burglary ring we were arrested for. And I was right about Bethanie and Cole, how he wasn't who he claimed to be and was totally scamming her," I say, reminding him of my most recent case. Which I single-handedly solved.

"You were only partly right about Cole," Marco says as he leans against a counter, arms crossed again. "I'm not saying you aren't good at this. I'm saying it's not your business. Take it to the cops if you suspect a crime. They have badges and guns and paychecks that prove crime-fighting is their job. You don't even have a driver's license yet."

"I will in less than two weeks. Have my license, I mean. When I turn sixteen," I say, which is probably the lamest thing I could have said.

"You kind of missed the point."

"I got the point. You're still mad I chose sleuthing over you."

"I'm not mad."

"And I didn't choose. It's just what I do. It's like asking me to choose between you and eating."

"Looking for trouble is not remotely the same as eating."

"It isn't even the sleuthing, is it?" I say, looking at all the photos on the refrigerator. "It's that I chose *anything* over you."

"Time's up, Chanti."

"It's probably a good thing we didn't work out," I say, getting up from the table myself and slinging my backpack over my shoulder. "You just don't get me, Marco."

"Maybe I don't. But I do get that you'll be studying for the French exam alone tonight, and I won't be."

I came up with a really evil response to that—on the walk home. When Marco immediately realized that what he said was too mean even if I did suggest he was kind of a diva, he tried to give me a ride home. I told him I didn't want him to miss Angelique's arrival and just walked out. Two hours ago when the tables were turned, I had looked back to see if he was watching me leave with Reginald. This time when I left, I glanced back but shouldn't have. He wasn't watching.

Chapter 8

The next morning, I consider faking sick to avoid seeing Marco at school, but at the last minute, change my mind. Gorgeous or not, best kisser on the planet or not, no guy is going to run my world. Lana is always telling me that no matter how much in love you are or how great a person he is, the sun does not rise and set on any boy, even if you're convinced it does.

What she hasn't taught me is how you make yourself believe that, but I figure this is one of those cases where it's best to fake it until you make it. Not to mention my academic situation is already a little sketchy since I've spent most of the semester preoccupied with little things like keeping myself out of jail and keeping Bethanie from showing up on a milk carton. Which is what I remind myself as I pass MJ's house on my walk to the bus stop. Her problems are not my problems.

I'm replaying that in my head, trying to turn it into a mantra, when I notice something shiny glinting in the lush green grass of Ada Crawford's yard. Yes, it's late November, but Ada gets her grass painted so it looks like springtime whether we're in the middle of winter or a drought. The sun is shining on the object in just the right way to make me think whatever it is, it's probably an expensive metal, not a beer bottle cap or a ball of tin foil.

I cross the street and walk across Ada's lawn, stopping a second to check out her house. Ada isn't Mrs. Jenkins, peeking through her curtains 24-7, but I want to make sure. The shiny object turns out to be a cigarette lighter, and not the plastic kind next to the register at the bodega. It's the old-fashioned kind like my grandfather has, a rectangle of silver with a flip top. And I mean real silver, not silver plated. There's a raised design on one side.

It'll give me the perfect excuse to try and get inside Ada's house so I can ask her a few questions, but considering her business hours, I doubt she's up this early. I slip the lighter into my pocket and continue toward the bus stop, reciting my MJ mantra. *Her problems are not my problems.* But you know what they say about best intentions—they are generally screwed the second you make them. Just as I reach Center Street, I hear someone yelling my name. Not just someone—it's MJ.

"Hold up," she says when she reaches me, a little out of breath. "Didn't you hear me calling you?"

"No. I'm running late for school and can't miss the next bus."

"You got a few minutes 'til the bus," she says, getting in step with me as I cross Center. "A person might think you trying to avoid them."

"That's exactly what a person should think when said person demanded I 'leave it alone.' And that's a quote."

"*It.* I said leave *it* alone, not me. You know these people on the street act like they can't say three words in my direction. If you stop talking to me, I won't have nobody that's got my back."

She says this just as we arrive at the bus shelter. Once there I recognize two riders who also live on Aurora Ave.

Since they're some of the people who don't have her back, she nods in their direction and raises her voice a little. For extra measure, she stares them down a couple of seconds, daring anyone to actually say three words to her. See, that's why I'm her only friend on the street. Hard to make friends when you're all the time acting like you're ready to jump bad on somebody. MJ could seriously use an anger management course, though I suppose this was probably a useful personality trait when she was serving time.

A bus arrives, but it isn't my route. Everyone else gets on, leaving MJ and me alone.

"Was Big Mama upset about the fire?"

"No. I told her it was an accident and she was just glad I was okay."

"Is she planning to file an insurance claim?"

"Why you asking that?"

"Just wondering. I mean, that's what people usually do when they have accidents. You'll probably need the fire report if you do."

"Nah, Big Mama said the small amount of damage ain't worth jacking up her premiums, plus the deductible is hella steep. She says there'd be questions about how it started and with me still on probation and everything—"

"Because she believes you started it."

"That's what she believes because that's what happened," MJ says, her voice full of threat.

"My bad, don't get all tense," I say, deciding on another approach. "So . . . you're up early this morning. You don't have your GED classes until the afternoon, right? That was one of the reasons you said you didn't want to go to regular high school, because the hours sucked."

"Yeah, that and after two years of high school courtesy of L.A. County juvie, I could care less about pep rallies and proms."

"You mean you *couldn't* care less."

"Exactly. Just want to finish my last semester and get my GED."

MJ also couldn't care less that she just did one of my pet peeves, so I go back to my questioning.

"The GED classes are from four to six, every weekday, is what I thought you told me."

"Yeah, but I have a job now. That's where I'm going. Eddie hooked me up with a part-time cashier job at the bodega."

I guess things are going well with Eddie, her new boyfriend and son of the Center Street bodega owner. I wonder what Eddie would think about Hoodie Dude.

"That's cool, except it must interfere with your classes."

"I only started yesterday, and I only work the morning shift. I open the store and leave at noon. I'm serious about getting my GED and never miss class."

"See, if I had a new job, at the end of my first day, I'd probably blow off my classes and go celebrate. Is that what you did yesterday between four and six?"

"I told you—I never miss school. Damn, Chanti. Why every other conversation with you gotta feel like I'm talking to my probie? Make me think maybe you *should* leave me alone. And why you so interested in my class work, anyway?"

"Just want to make sure you get that diploma. Like you said, I got your back," I remind her as I fish my bus pass out of my bag.

"Well, if that's true, maybe you could help me with my math homework."

I'm thinking a tutoring session would be the perfect opportunity to do some snooping at her house when she adds, "Meet me at Treets at seven? Since I'm making a little cash now, I'll buy."

"Why not your house?"

"It still smells like smoke. Probably a health hazard."

"Then why are you and Big Mama still living there?"

"Where else would we go?"

I don't get a chance to answer her because my bus pulls up just then. MJ might think she's just been saved by the crosstown, but I have other plans.

I was at Langdon Prep less than a month when Lana discovered I could get into trouble—through no fault of my own—whether I'm at a fancy school across town or at my nearby public school. And as much as I hated Langdon, I told Lana I'd stay when she gave me a chance to leave my scholarship and transfer back to North Denver Heights. I guess I owe Michelle an apology because when school started, I accused her of going to a school because a boy she liked went there, and I ended up choosing to stay at a school for the same reason. I turned down Lana's offer because Marco and I were still an item and I had an ally in Bethanie, the other scholarship girl. Now that she's moved away, I realize I'm going to have to make new friends, especially since Reginald won't arrive for another six weeks. Otherwise Langdon will be unbearable for the next year and a half.

That's why I look for Annette Park in the cafeteria at lunch. I probably hold the title of least-liked girl at Langdon, but Annette is definitely a contender. If you know our history, you might think she'd be the person most likely to start a campaign to get me expelled. But politics make strange bedfellows, and everyone knows politics don't get any stranger—or more ruthless—than they are in high school.

I find Annette alone at the table where she and her crew used to hold court over the whole school before I brought down their leader. I fully expect her to haul off and slap me, or at least knock my tray out of my hands, so I'm completely thrown when she looks up and smiles. If Headmistress Smythe hadn't already expelled Annette's former queen bee, I'd be pretty worried right about now. As it is, I instinctively look around the cafeteria for signs of impending foul play. But everything seems normal, like any other school cafeteria, except today's menu includes pâté on crostini and hand-tossed goat cheese pizza. It's my favorite place at Langdon—not a fish stick to be found and I'm sure they've never served those cheese-covered cardboard rectangles they tried to pass off as pizza at my old school.

"Can I sit here?" I ask, still a little wary.

"Yeah, but why would you? Don't you hate me? Everyone else does, and you're the only one with a reason to."

She's got a point, but before I can explain myself, she starts talking again.

"I'm not really like her, you know. I mean, like Lissa Mitchell," she explains, invoking the name of the she-beast that caused me nothing but grief from the day I set foot on campus.

"Where are the other two—Lissa's clones? Why don't you guys have lunch together anymore?" I ask.

It's something I've been wondering about from the minute Headmistress Smythe had to admit her favorite student had violated more than a few of Langdon's rules of conduct and had to throw her out. It was even more painful for Smythe because she originally accused me of committing the violations until I cleared my name. Smythe never liked me from the get-go, thanks to how she met my mother—during one of Lana's undercover jobs in which Smythe somehow became indebted to my mom. I know Smythe thinks Lana is a convict and by default, I'm just a crime away from my own prison sentence. There's more to it than that, of course, but Lana won't tell me what actually went down between them—a mystery for another day.

"If they're anything like me, they're somewhere having lunch alone, just like they did B.L."

"Huh?"

"B.L. *Before Lissa.*"

Wow. I used to call the girls in Lissa's crew her minions, but maybe *disciples* would have been more appropriate.

"When was that?" I ask, spreading goose liver and capers on little toasts. It sounds gross, but it's sooo good. Rich people know how to eat.

"When I was a freshman. Every year, Lissa picked three new freshmen to be in her circle."

"So after a year, she fired you from your job as lackey? No offense."

"I've had some time to think about it since practically no one talks to me now. That's exactly what we were—her lackeys. Lissa looked for easy marks, girls who don't yet know who they are and could easily be convinced to become someone else. Where better to find those girls than in freshman class? Only freshmen were crazy enough to do her bidding, so she had to get a new batch every year when the last recruits figured her out."

"But you're a junior."

"I guess I was the easiest mark of all. Two years later and I still don't know who I am," she says, then adds a weak smile, the kind people make when they want you to think it's all good but it really isn't.

"Let's not talk about Lissa anymore," I say. And because we have nothing else in common to talk about, we finish our goat cheese pizza mostly in silence. But sometimes silence is just right.

Chapter 9

When MJ arrives at Tastee Treets at seven on the dot, she finds me in the same booth she and Hoodie Dude shared yesterday. Maybe sitting here will unnerve her and trip her up on the lie she told me. After all, I saw her having burgers with him. I'm sitting in her same spot, facing the front exit so I can see her and anyone else who comes through the door—a habit I picked up from Lana.

"Hey, you picked my favorite booth," MJ says as she drops her heavy math textbook on the table with a thud. So much for unnerving her. "I'll order for us. Super Combo Three, right?"

I nod, thinking MJ is a good study of people, even if she doesn't always use the information wisely. She already knows I'm not very adventurous with the Tastee Treets menu—I almost always order the Super Combo #3: quarter-pound burger with cheese, fries, and a chocolate shake. MJ is almost as good as Lana at reading me when I'm running a game, even better than my BF Tasha and she's known me forever. That makes my job tough so by the time she returns with our food, I've decided on the straightforward approach.

"I know you told me to leave it alone, MJ, but I really think we should tell the police about that guy I saw."

"You supposed to be helping me with my math home-work. If you just gonna question me about some guy you think is an arsonist, I want eight dollars for that Super Combo."

"I can't help you with your homework until we're done eating or our food will get cold, and we have to talk about something while we eat, right?"

"We don't have to talk about that. Besides, what would you tell the cops? 'I saw some guy watching the fire along with the rest of the street and I'm thinking he's a criminal be-cause I've never seen him before'? Yeah, I'm sure they'll jump right on that."

"I can give them more than that. I have a description," I say, watching MJ's face for a reaction as she squirts an obscene amount of ketchup on her fries. I get nothing, so I continue. "He was approximately five-eight or five-nine, a hundred and sixty pounds, medium complexion, between eighteen and twenty-four years of age."

"Do you know how much like a cop you sound? It's kind of funny" is the only reaction I get from MJ. "Not to mention that could be just about anyone."

"He was wearing a brown hoodie with an elaborate white scroll design across the back. . . ."

Now MJ stops scarfing down her fries and looks up at me. I finally got her attention.

". . . and I think I saw writing on it . . ."

Now she stops mid-chew and looks more than a little worried.

". . . maybe the numbers oh-four."

I'm not ready to show my full hand yet so I don't men-tion what I actually saw. She relaxes enough to start chewing again, but I can tell she's thinking about it, wondering what to say next.

"Oh hell, I know who you talking about now. You

should've gave me the 411 on Sunday and we could have avoided all this threatening-to-go-to-the-cops drama."

"I didn't make any threats. I just thought you'd want to catch the guy that might be responsible for trying to burn down your grandma's house."

"You mean my boyfriend?" she says.

"Eddie? I know for sure it wasn't Eddie. He's like six-two, way taller than Hoodie Dude."

"No, I mean Lux."

"What? I'm confused."

"The guy you've been calling Hoodie Dude, the arsonist, etcetera. His name is Lux and he's my man."

"I thought Eddie and you were   "

"I know what you thought and I keep saying you're wrong. Eddie and me are just friends."

"But what about . . . you know?"

"Okay, so Eddie comes with benefits."

I don't know what to make of this new development, so I'm inclined to think she's lying. Guilty until proven innocent is the way I see it.

"You've never mentioned Lux before."

"I don't tell you all my business. You already find out enough without my help."

"How long have you been going out? I mean, maybe you don't know him as well as you think."

MJ looks like she wants to tell me to shut the hell up and eat, but I guess she's been my friend long enough to know that if she doesn't give me answers, I'll go find some on my own, and possibly the wrong ones.

"I known him long enough to know he's the last person who wants to see my house burn down, and I mean the *very* last. He called 911."

"I told you it was me who called."

"Probably lots of people call 911 when there's a fire."

That's true, if it's a blazing fire. I suppose people in the houses behind MJ's may have seen the smoke and called, but Lux was out front when I noticed him. Of course, I was kind of busy yelling for MJ and Big Mama, ringing doorbells and banging on *rejas* before I spotted him in Ada's yard. Maybe that's when he was calling 911. I take a long drag of chocolate shake while I consider this.

"Before Lux and I left the house that morning—"

"He was over *that* early?"

"Like I said, he's my man," MJ says, looking suddenly smug, like she's just discovered the proof that will finally convince me Lux couldn't be the firestarter. "Big Mama was out of town, so Lux stayed over. Anyway, before we left, I put some fireplace embers from the night before on the back porch. I guess they wasn't as cooled off as I thought. That's probably what started the fire."

"Seriously? You accidentally started the fire with hot embers?"

"You say it like I'm stupid. I'm not the only person that ever started a fire like that. Besides, I'm from southern Cal— what I know about cleaning a fireplace?" MJ says, looking at me like she's trying to will me to believe her, and I do. *I* may not believe hot embers were the cause of the fire, but MJ does. "People always think I'm stupid."

"Okay," I say, feeling guilty, "so you put out the embers and headed to work, but Lux says he called 911. I thought he'd left the house with you?"

"Yeah, so?"

"So why was he still there to see the fire and make the call?"

"He must have left something at my place and came back to get it."

"You don't know? Seems like y'all would have discussed the fire by now. It's been a couple days."

"No, we discussed it," MJ says, not looking as smug as she

did a second ago. "He definitely came back to the house for something and that's when he noticed the smoke."

"How was he going to get inside? I know Big Mama wouldn't let him have a key to her house. She'd kill you and then kick you out if you gave him one."

"I don't know. I guess . . . maybe I forgot to lock up and he noticed that."

I let that one slide because I'm on a roll and MJ is starting to crack.

"All right. He comes back, notices the smoke, calls the fire department. So why did he leave when you got there?"

"Huh?" MJ says, sounding genuinely confused.

"He was standing in Ada's yard before you got home from the bodega. I talked to you a few minutes, then I spotted him walking toward Center Street. If you're his girlfriend, wouldn't he stick around long enough to talk to you, make sure you were okay?"

"I'm getting tired of you interrogating me like I'm in the box, Chanti," MJ says, and I know she's stalling, thinking up an explanation. "Only reason I'm putting up with you is I need help with my math and I know you'll just snoop until you find out, anyway."

"True dat."

"Lux didn't stay around because he knows I'm creeping on Eddie."

"Eddie, who isn't your boyfriend?"

"Okay, okay—I'm seeing them both. I'm eighteen, too young to be with just one dude."

I almost feel bad grilling MJ like this because her eyes are starting to have the cornered-animal look, but I can't tell the truth from the lies. Like she said, she recently turned eighteen and if she does time now, it'll be for real, no more juvie. If she's on her way down a path that might take her back to jail, my interrogation will help more than hurt my friend. At the very least, she's hanging out with a Down Home—a fact I still haven't let on I know—and that alone is a violation of her probation. On the other hand, a cornered animal can be dangerous if they think the only way out is to attack, so I tread lightly but don't pull my punch.

"If Lux is a good guy and cares about you, why was he smiling as he watched the fire? And why would he stop smiling when the fire trucks arrived?"

This news was the final assault and I wait for MJ to go on the attack, so I'm surprised when she just deflates like I've let all the air out of her. Half her story may still be a lie, but she truly believed she started the fire. I may have finally convinced her Lux may not be who she thinks he is; this last information was the piece she was missing to put two and two together. But the confused expression on her face as she pours half the bottle of ketchup on her burger makes me think everything just added up to five.

When I get home from TasteeTreets, I find Lana there. I'd hoped to beat her home, but after that interrogation, I spent an hour helping MJ with her geometry.

"Where have you been?" Lana asks. "It's almost nine o'clock."

"I thought you had a late stakeout."

"That doesn't answer my question."

"MJ needed help with her homework so we met up at TasteeTreets. Look—I brought you a fish dinner."

Lana takes the bag from me and says, "Ooh, still hot." Lecture averted.

After she pours herself some iced tea and brings a bottle of malt vinegar to the table, I figure it's a good time to pick her brain. Lana is always happy when there's an order of Tastee's fried catfish and hush puppies in front of her, so I'm hoping all that greasy goodness will camouflage any questions about my new case. MJ really believed she started the fire, and she may even be messing around with Lux since he is a member of her former gang, but there were many lies woven in with the truth.

"Did you find out anything new about the fire at MJ's house?" I ask Lana.

"No, too early for the report to be filed."

"You think you could check on the 911 calls, too?"

"What are you up to, Chanti?"

"I was just curious about the response time. You know how you said the nearest fire truck should get to our house four minutes after dispatch?"

"Yeah?" Lana says, slowing down on her fish dinner. Yep, I figured this would be the right lie to tell.

"Well, it seemed a lot longer than that to me, more like seven or eight minutes. And you know more than one person usually calls in a house fire. If someone called in before me, that means the response time was even longer."

"It had better not be eight minutes, unless the city wants a lawsuit. I'll check the call records, too."

There won't be any lawsuits because the report will show the firefighters arrived when they were supposed to, but that little lie was extra insurance Lana would pull the information for me.

"You never can be too careful," I say, mostly as a reminder to myself of how to approach my next question for Lana. "So, don't you have something you want to discuss with me?"

"What?" Lana says all innocent, like she actually has no idea.

"You promised. You said you'd tell me everything you know about my father—the reason we don't want him in our lives, why you changed our phone number."

"Not now, Chanti. I've got some work to do," she says, getting up from the table and hurriedly putting the rest of her food in the refrigerator. That means she's really trying to avoid me because she always finishes the fish dinner combo. "I'll be in my office the rest of the night."

"Mom, what are you hiding from me?"

"Don't you have homework to do?" she asks, her back turned to me as she pauses before leaving the kitchen.

"That doesn't answer my question."

"Better watch yourself," Lana says without giving me the evil eye that usually goes with that threat. Now she can't even look at me when I ask about him.

Chapter 10

Coffee. I don't want to see, hear, or think about anything else right now. I didn't fall asleep until three in the morning when my body finally overtook my brain. I couldn't stop worrying about MJ and Lux, my mother's refusal to tell me what's going on, and last but surprisingly least—Marco. Maybe I'm actually getting over him if I'm willing to put him last on my list of things to worry about. And as if I'm somehow putting that vibe out into the universe, a text from Reginald woke me up this morning. He seems like a nice guy, and definitely nice to look at, but for now, I ignore his offer to hang out this weekend. I have enough to deal with. Hey, Universe—if you're listening, I said I'm *getting* over Marco, as in, still working on it.

The coffeemaker is just gasping out its last puff of steam when I get to the kitchen, but there's no Lana. She wasn't in the bathroom, either. I checked her bedroom and found the bed made. We don't have one of those fancy coffeemakers that you can program, just an ancient Mr. Coffee that was a housewarming gift when Lana moved into her first apartment years ago. She must have dashed when she heard me up. I find a note propped against the coffeemaker. It's so freshly written that I smudge the ink when I pick it up.

Have an early meeting this morning, and don't expect to be back until after you're asleep tonight. Don't wait up. Left $20 on the kitchen table—order a pizza and keep what's left.

Translation: *I'm avoiding you, Chanti. And also bribing you with pizza and change.* That's okay. I'll give her a break until the weekend when she'll have nowhere to run. I'm avoiding Reginald's text, so I'm guilty too.

The coffee raised me enough from the dead that I was able to shower, dress, and get out the door in time to catch my bus, but not enough to keep me from being uncoordinated. I stumbled over the threshold as I walked out onto the porch, spilling the contents of my unzipped backpack. As I'm down on hands and knees trying to find a lip gloss that rolled behind a planter full of long-dead mums, I hear voices coming from Mrs. Jenkins's house. No, a little farther away than that, and it's a guy's voice. I don't think Mrs. Jenkins has had a guy at her house since Mr. Jenkins passed away seven years ago, which is probably why she's so mean. I stand up to see MJ on her porch talking to Lux.

I back up to my door so they can't see me. I can't make out the words, but Lux's voice is angry. I step back out onto the porch enough to watch them and hope they're so deep in conversation that they don't catch me spying. Okay, so it isn't exactly a conversation. Lux is doing all the talking, though it sounds more like the kind of yelling you do when you don't want anyone to overhear. When he puts his finger in MJ's face, I'm expecting her to break it along with his arm because MJ has a good four inches and forty pounds on Lux, not to mention she's an all-around badass. So I'm shocked when she not only backs away from him, she starts talking so softly to him that I can't hear her voice at all, making gestures like she's trying to explain herself. MJ Cooper does nothing softly, and apologizes to no one even if she probably should. Lux must be satisfied with MJ's response, because now he's walking to his car.

Before I leave the porch, I wait a few minutes to make sure Lux is long gone and MJ is inside her house. My bus is also long gone, but it's worth missing most of first period to have caught this scene. Now I know for sure that MJ is lying about Lux being her side dude.

I'm at my locker between second and third periods reading a note from Reginald. He must have had his mom stick the note through the slots because it wasn't here before second period and unless he's skipping, he should be in class at North Denver Heights right now.

Sorry for the old-school approach, but I think I must have your number wrong.

Uh no, I'm just evil and ignored your texts.

Doing anything this weekend? I have tickets to a Broncos game. Hit me up if you'd like to go.

Three hours in the cold watching a sport I don't like. Now that I'm not with Marco, I never want to endure that torture again. See what I mean about the things a cute boy will make you do?

"Hey, Chanti. You got a second?"

It's Marco. I'm serious about that whole Universe thing. I really believe it has a LoJack on my love life. I throw the note into my locker guiltily, as though just being near it Marco will know I'm talking to another guy. As though he'd even care.

"That's about all I have," I say, pointing to my wrist and an imaginary watch. "Third-period bell is about to ring."

"What I said the other day before you left my house . . . that was out of bounds. I shouldn't have—"

"It's okay, Marco. This whole thing is kind of weird, but we'll get used to it. Seriously—no worries."

"This isn't just about my parents hating you, or me not wanting you to play detective. It's about the attention you tend to attract—cop attention—that my family doesn't need right now."

"Is something going on?"

"I told you about my cousin living with us."

"Your cousin?"

Marco looks at me like I should know exactly why his cousin should have anything to do with whether we're together or not.

"Remember, not long after we first met? I told you my cousin David's parents had recently been deported and how he was supposed to go, too, but my aunt and uncle brought him to us before INS took them away. When we were dealing with the whole school burglary ring and Donnell, I told you then I couldn't have the cops in my business."

"Oh, right. I forgot about David. You hadn't talked about him since that first time, so I thought everything must have worked out."

"How could it work out? The INS fairies let his parents back into the country and they lived happily ever after? The immigration laws magically changed? You say I want to be the center of everything, but you should check yourself, Chanti."

While I may concede his point, how is this conversation going any better than the one he came to apologize for?

"You could have just reminded me that was the real reason you had to break up with me instead of saying your parents think I'm dangerous."

"It was kind of a big deal, at least to me and my family. I didn't think you'd forget it. You remember every little detail about your investigations, but can't remember a huge one about me."

Ouch.

Marco continues, "Anyway, I kinda regret I told you in the first place. It was a slip. The fewer people know David's undocumented, going to school when he was supposed to be deported, the better. Besides, if I'd reminded you, would you have dropped the whole Bethanie and Cole investigation? Would you stop trying to track down this guy you think is an arsonist?"

I'm quiet, trying to think of a way to tell him he's right, but not because I don't care about him.

Before I come up with the right words, Marco turns to leave and I hear him say, "Yeah, that's what I thought."

Chapter 11

Instead of heading home after the bus drops me off, I make a stop at the Center Street bodega to check if MJ is lying about her new boyfriend or not. If she wasn't lying about never missing school, she should be in class right now and Eddie should be working the cash register.

The day started out cold, but the sun has made the afternoon warm enough to bring people out, including Crazy Moses, who is standing outside the bodega leaning against his shopping cart/home, money cup in hand. I have to tell him twice that I'm not working at TasteeTreets anymore and can't give him free coffee like I used to. I actually had to pay for it with my employee discount, but I always told him it was free. Moses didn't get the Crazy added on to his name for no reason. Half-priced coffee was a small price to pay to keep things peaceful during my shift at the register whenever he was there. Now I can't afford to subsidize him.

Moses being here tips me off that Eddie's father isn't working today. Mr. Perez would never let Moses hang around his door harassing his customers like that. Eddie doesn't care. He's just killing time while he figures out what's next. He was recently kicked out of college for being a slacker and never showing up for class, and his father is making him work in the bodega to earn his keep. Eddie couldn't care less about his father's store and is probably the last person to be trusted with it, but MJ made me promise to stay out of their family business. She's got a point—I have my own father issues to deal with. But that doesn't mean I'm staying out of MJ's business when doing so could mean letting my friend get herself into a world of trouble.

"Tamale girl," Eddie says when I walk into the store, like he's announcing the queen.

"It's Chanti," I say.

"Yeah, I know—MJ's friend. But you usually only come in on Freebie Friday for the buy-one-get-one tamales."

It's true, and apparently I've got an easy-to-mark pattern even though Eddie hasn't been working in the bodega very long. I need to work on that—not a good trait for a detective, even one who isn't really a detective. Now I'll have to buy something to keep my cover. Good thing I took Lana's twenty off the table this morning, not that I plan on spending more than I have to. There's an extra-cheese-and-pepperoni pizza calling my name right now.

"I come in other times, like now, when I get off the bus from school."

"Yeah? I must not have been working those other times," Eddie says.

If it was anyone else, I'd think he was reading me, but from what MJ has told me, Eddie didn't just fail in college because he was a slacker. He probably believes me and really thinks he wasn't working those times, even though this is his regular shift.

"You have any Bubble Yum?" I ask. "I wanted to buy some for MJ because I'm always mooching off her. You know what her favorite flavor is?"

"Really? I've never seen MJ with gum."

He's right; it is a bad cover story. He's reading my habits

and my lies—I'm way off my game. Thanks to Marco messing with my head. And my heart.

"It was only once or twice I bummed off her. It's not like
she has a Bubble Yum addiction or anything."

"Well, I know she likes grape slushes."

"You know MJ pretty well, don't you?" I say, finally getting the opening I was so ineptly looking for. "Things must
be going great for y'all, huh?"

"Oh yeah, me and MJ are definitely tight. I never thought
she'd be my kind of girl, her being all roughneck and everything. I was chasing pretty girls around campus and didn't
know what a real woman would be like."

Unbelievably, he says this all dreamy-like. I suppress a
smile.

"MJ is about as real as it gets," I say, putting the pack of
grape gum, two protein bars, and Lana's twenty on the
counter.

"Yeah. Ain't nothing pink and frilly about her. You never
know what you want until it hits you."

"*It* hits you? You mean like—"

"Nah, man . . . it's like . . . you know," he says.

Like most guys, he fumbles the four-letter L word like it
can't possibly relate to him, so I let him off the hook.

"Right, I know. And MJ won't ever hear it from me," I
promise as he gives me my change.

On my way out, I give Crazy Moses the protein bars. I'll
probably regret it the next time I see him when I'll have to
explain why I can't give him free coffee *or* Power Bars now.

"You can pay me back when you have a little extra," I tell
him, hoping he'll remember I said it and won't expect free-
bies whenever he sees me. I know he'll never have a little
extra. Some panhandlers probably make more than I ever did
at Treets, but Crazy Moses isn't one of them. People generally
cross the street to avoid him; he scares off too many people to
actually make any money.

"Not to worry," he says and nods, taking the bars. I'm never sure what this means because, outside of demanding money, food, or coffee from people, I've never heard Moses say anything but those three words. He says them all the time, whether he's pushing his cart up the street, panhandling on the corner, or sitting on the sidewalk in front of Seoul BBQ enjoying someone's donated leftovers—you'll hear him repeating those same three words over and over. I always figured he was trying to convince himself, not the rest of us, but sometimes I wonder.

I should take Moses's advice, but that'll never happen. Right now, I'm worried about MJ. Either she's lying about things between her and Eddie not being serious or the poor guy is completely deluded. The way he kept looking all stupid-in-love whenever I mentioned MJ, that delusion theory is not improbable. But there are other ways to get information than from the source, and sometimes they're even more reliable than the source. This is especially true when a would-be informant thinks of gossip as a sport and she's training for the gold. On my walk home, I call in a pizza order and then text Tasha to come over for a slice in about fifteen minutes.

Before I go home, I make a stop at Ada Crawford's house, the weight of the heavy lighter reminding me that it's been in my coat pocket—and on my mind—for a couple of days. After I explain I might have found something of Ada's to her housekeeper, who I am certain is the only one working on Aurora Avenue and probably a five-block radius, I am shown into the house. I only have a second to get over the surprise of actually being let in before I am struck by the house itself. Like with my first visit to Marco's place, Ada's house is nothing like I had imagined, which involved leather furniture, feather boas, and black lights. Or at least something like her car, a gold Lexus with gold medallions, gold spinners, and gold everything else. Instead, it looks like someone forced Ada to only shop at Laura Ashley for the rest of her days. Pastel flowers bloom on the walls, curtains, pillows—everywhere.

While I wait for Ada in the foyer—she actually has one and again, I'm sure it's the only one on the block—I look around for clues that she is who I have always suspected she is despite her sweet and innocent interior design. Like maybe a guestbook with all her clients' names that I could sneak a peek at like they always do in the movies. But I guess it isn't like she's running a bed and breakfast, even though her décor might suggest it.

"You have something for me?"

I turn around to find Ada dressed the same way she does on those rare times I run into her around the neighborhood—normal. No leather bras or those little shoes with the feathers on front. I really watch too much TV, and possibly the wrong kind.

"Well, I'm not sure it's yours."

"So why would you come see me about it?"

"Because I found it on your—on the sidewalk in front of your house."

"What is it?"

"I was wondering if, uh, you could tell me," I say, a little nervous. Something about Ada is intimidating, even surrounded by pale flowers. Maybe because she's really pretty, even prettier than everyone on the street thinks she is, when you get up close. Or maybe because I know what she does in this house of flowers. "I thought if one of your, uh, visitors had lost something, you could describe it to me. It probably would have been last Sunday—likely Saturday night—that they lost it."

"So whatever it is," Ada says, smiling a little, "you're suggesting it's something a man would own."

"Yes, that's what I'm suggesting. Ma'am."

"No, none of my visitors have lost anything. Could I have a look at it, anyway?"

Reluctantly, I fish the lighter out of my pocket and instead of handing it to her, hold it up for her to see. I don't know why I think she's going to take it, but . . .

"Hey!" I say as she grabs it from me.

"This is nice," she says, appraising like she's looking at a diamond through a jeweler's loupe. "What do you think this design on it is?"

"Um, I have no idea," I say as I snatch the lighter back.

"I wasn't going to steal it," Ada says, looking to me like she was totally planning to steal it. Then she gives me a hard once-over. "What's your story anyway, little girl? And your mother. I always wondered about her game, though I have my suspicions."

"We, I mean me and my mother, we always wondered about your game, too. We have our suspicions, too. Ma'am."

"I suppose we should both just keep our suspicions to ourselves. You know, let sleeping dogs lie."

Uh, it's confirmed. Ada Crawford weirds me out.

"Okay, well, thanks about the lighter," I say, "but I gotta go. I have a pizza being delivered."

She says something to me, but I don't hear it because I'm out the door and down the steps before she can even finish her sentence.

"Hey, girl," Tasha says when I open my front door. "This pizza offer was right on time. My parents are doing a date night and I was going to have to fend for myself. Kinda early for dinner though, isn't it?"

"Yeah, but I figured we could catch up. It's been a while."

"Glad you noticed. Since you started going to that new school, we never get to talk."

"I know, but between the crazy amount of homework they give me and the bus commute, I don't have much time left."

Not to mention all the time I spend crime-solving, but I

leave that part off. I'm dying to tell her about my visit to Ada's house, but it's best to keep investigation details under wraps unless you need to reveal them. Instead, I fill her in on my breakup with Marco and show off the new birthday dress I have no place to wear since I haven't made plans and don't have a date. Tasha shares the latest news about people I knew at my old school and what's going on around the Ave.

Which brings me to MJ.

"So what's the word on MJ and Eddie?" I ask Tasha as I refill our glasses with soda. "Are they still together?"

"She's *your* friend. You ought to know."

"We don't talk much anymore."

"I saw y'all talking when her house was on fire. Speaking of, what's up with that? Do they know how it started?" Tasha asks, completely turning the interviewing table on me.

"MJ thought it might be embers from her fireplace that she left on the back porch."

"Who puts out hot embers? She ain't too bright, is she? I guess they don't have too many fireplaces in Los Angeles. Maybe now she'll leave Aurora Ave and go back there."

"Because she accidentally started a fire?" I say, even though I still don't believe MJ started the fire even if MJ does.

"That and the fact she's involved with Eddie Perez."

"They hooked up?"

"You didn't know?" Tasha asks, taking another slice from the pizza box. "Yeah, they're real tight."

"So why would she go back to Los Angeles if she's in tight with Eddie? Are they having problems?"

"They aren't, but he might cause some for MJ. She's on parole and not supposed to be associating with criminals."

"Eddie isn't a criminal."

"But his dad might be real soon. I heard he might go into business with Big Mama, running Numbers out of his store."

"MJ lives in the same house as Big Mama. She can get

into trouble from the Numbers game without any help from Eddie and his family."

"It's different when it's your relative. The cops will figure she couldn't help that—who she's related to and where she lives," Tasha says, lowering her voice. "She *can* help who her boyfriend is and who he hangs with."

Whenever Tasha starts gossiping, her voice gets quieter and all conspiratorial even if we're the only ones in the house. I don't bother to tell her she's wrong about how cops will see it. I take the bait instead.

"So who's he hanging out with?"

"You won't believe this, but Michelle has started talking to Cisco."

Tasha says the name like I should know who that is. My face must register clueless.

"Chanti, you really do need to keep up with what's going on in your own neighborhood."

"Not when I can get all the gossip from you. So who is he?"

"He was Donnell Down-the-Street's second man."

"How many men did he have?"

"Well, just the one—Cisco. Now that DTS is in jail, it looks like Cisco is taking over his operation."

I know about Donnell DTS since I helped put him in jail, but I didn't know about a second man. I thought Donnell was a small-time dealer trying to go big thanks to MJ's gang connections. When I stopped those plans, I thought I'd taken out an Aurora Avenue criminal for good. I swear, they're just like roaches. Step on one, here come two more.

"Let's go back to Michelle and her really bad taste in guys. How is Eddie connected to Cisco?"

"They aren't yet, but Cisco is trying to get in on Big Mama's Numbers game, too. He figures if he can make friends with Eddie, he can get Eddie to talk his dad into join-ing up with Big Mama. Then Cisco would be in on the ground floor."

My neighborhood criminals are an entrepreneurial bunch! But if Eddie and his dad haven't joined the dark side, maybe I can find a way to help them stay straight. I mean, right after I figure out what's up with MJ and her mystery man, and why my mother is so afraid to tell me about the man known as my father.

After Tasha and I dish on Michelle and her questionable boyfriend choices over the last of the pizza, she heads home. I wait half an hour before I walk over to Michelle's place, when I know Tasha will be glued to the TV and *Entertainment Tonight*. She even loves gossip about people she doesn't know. Tasha could have been helpful in getting Michelle to open up, but she knows me too well not to know I'm snooping. I still think it's best to keep my investigation on the quiet until I figure out what MJ is lying about, because I know she's lying about something.

By now it's dark out, but even before I walk down my steps I can see people standing on Michelle's porch, thanks to a full moon and her porch light being turned on. Instead of going over there, I stay out of sight and watch from behind a minivan parked on my side of the street. I've spotted Michelle and I'm wondering if one of the two guys is Cisco. If they move a little closer to the porch light, I'll be able to get a good look at his face. I'll probably need to have a conversation with him at some point, scary as that sounds. Then one guy shifts, turning his back to the street, and wouldn't you know—he's wearing that same damn hoodie, all lit up like the moon is his personal spotlight.

Chapter 12

It's a good thing I don't have a driver's license yet, or a car, because after three nights in a row of almost zero sleep, I would be a menace on the road. As it is, I'm a danger to myself. I haven't even left the house and I've already required bandages (cut my finger slicing a bagel), an ice water bath for the other hand (poured hot coffee on it while trying to get some into a cup), and tripped over my own feet twice. All because I was awake most of the night worried about MJ and who she may or may not be seeing. If she's going out with someone who'd hang out with an associate of Donnell DTS, then she's in trouble. Before I helped bust him, Donnell was using MJ to get connected to her old gang. Now she's into something with Lux. MJ's saved my butt a few times, and it's more than a theory that I need to save her from herself. And the penal system.

Lana did another disappearing act on me this morning, still in evasion mode. There's another twenty on the table, but no note this time. I guess she figures by now I know the game she's playing. Under the twenty is a manila folder. With the few uninjured fingers I have left, I open it to find the report from MJ's house fire. What I find in it doesn't help me at all. In fact, the report puts the final touch on what has already been a very bad day and it isn't even seven o'clock in the morning. The report confirms what MJ has been telling me all along—the fire was started by hot embers igniting a flammable substance on the back porch.

At the end of seventh period, I find Marco waiting outside my classroom. I see him before he spots me in the crowd of kids trying to squeeze out the door at the same time. It's the last class of the last day before Thanksgiving break, so it's crazy in the hallway right now. He's leaning against a row of lockers, his tie already loosened at the neck, the top button of his oxford shirt undone. He makes dress code violation look very good. I wonder how he managed to get out of his last class before bell.

As he watches the crowd in the doorway, just the idea of him looking for me makes my heart race—even if it's just because he wants to copy my French notes or something academic. Even if he turned the tables on me and called me out as the one who's self-absorbed. When he catches my eye, he smiles and my poor heart can barely take it. Bad hormones, bad. *Can't have him, we're just friends. Can't have him, we're just friends.* I figure if I repeat this enough times, I'll eventually believe it.

"Hey, I'm glad I caught you," he says when I finally make my way across the hall through the throng of kids. "Look, Chanti, after the way our last two conversations have gone, I'd understand if you're avoiding me. But I don't want you to." He reaches out to touch my face but pulls his hand back at the last minute, then laughs awkwardly. "I mean, we're not together, but we can still be friends, right? We were friends first."

"Technically we were friends at least twice as long as we were more than that. The other part was so short we could pretend it never happened."

"No, it happened," he says, and damn if he doesn't look at

me that way that makes me crazy for him. "It would probably still be happening if . . . well, I guess that's old news, right?"

"Right."

"The main thing I wanted to tell you is we can still hang out. I can give you a ride home tonight if you need one, but you'd have to kill some time before and after."

As much as I could just stand there and listen to Marco talk about, oh, anything, he is making no sense at all. "Before and after *what?*" I ask.

"The game tonight. You're coming, right?"

"I completely forgot there was a game." What is it with guys and football? Okay, so Marco actually plays, but that's one perk of us being just friends—I no longer have to go to his games. Which reminds me—I need to text Reginald. "Won't Angelique be there to cheer you on?"

"Yeah, she's coming," Marco says, looking a little disappointed if I'm reading him right. I read just about everybody right except Marco. He makes it hard for me to be objective. "I just thought maybe you'd be there, too. It would be nice to see another friendly face in the stands when I make the game-winning touchdown."

"Oh, I see you have big plans. Does the other team know?"

"They will in about four hours. So I can't talk you into staying?"

He probably could if I didn't have to watch him leave with another girl. But wait—he's offering me a ride home.

"If I stayed, Angelique probably wouldn't appreciate you leaving with me."

"I'm giving her a ride home, too."

"What?"

"She'll get a ride to the game, then we can all leave together. We all have to go to Denver Heights anyway."

Seriously, are guys really this clueless? As much as I hate to admit, the two times I've been around Angelique, she seemed genuinely nice. But even the nicest girl won't want to include a thirty-minute ride with her boyfriend and his ex on her date-night agenda.

"And you think this is a good idea because . . . ?"

"I think Angelique would be more comfortable with the idea of you and I being friends if she could meet you, I mean really meet you."

Comfortable. Now it hits me why Marco always goes back to Angelique and why the most we can hope for is 'just friends.' She's *comfortable*, not remotely dangerous, and his parents probably love her. Angelique is the anti-Chanti.

"I imagine Angelique isn't loving our platonic friendship thing," I say, already knowing the answer. I don't blame her. No girl is that nice, and I'll suspect any who claim to be.

"Yeah, but I don't want this to be a problem."

"Neither do I, which is why I'd better stick to my original plans for the night. Too many people in your world have beef with me, Marco. First your parents, now your girlfriend. And I totally get why Angelique has beef—I was the same way when we were together and you were still friends with her."

"So you have plans for tonight?" Marco asks, apparently only hearing the first part of what I just said.

Suddenly I feel brave, or at least fool myself into thinking I do, and say the thing I've wanted to ever since he reminded me about his cousin.

"Marco, you were right the other day. About David, I mean. I wouldn't have stopped sleuthing, but not because it's more important to me than you. It's *just as* important, and not because I get my thrills from it. It's because I can help people. Just like you're helping your cousin. And now I totally get why being with me can cause your family problems. Maybe even just being friends is dangerous."

"No, just friends is good," Marco says, taking my hand and holding it for just a second before letting go. "Someone has to look out for you. You keep doing this detective thing, at some point, you're going to get into trouble. I don't have to like it, but at least I'll know what you're up to."

"Thanks," I say, and kiss him lightly on the cheek. It isn't much, but now that I know this is it, that there's no more possibility of us being together, regardless of how much I daydream about him during chemistry class or on the bus rides home—or all the time —I need a good-bye kiss.

"I won't see you until after the break, I guess."

"I guess," I say, realizing maybe we're both going to have a hard time adjusting to our new and confirmed status.

"A week is a lot of time for you to get into some kind of trouble . . . you know, that whole situation with your friend MJ."

"I'll be fine. Maybe I'll have it solved by the time we come back from break."

"You probably will. But if you need help or get into something, hit me up, okay? I'll be around."

He turns to leave, heading for the gym.

"Good luck tonight," I say, but he's too far away to hear me.

It wasn't a lie when I told Marco I had plans, but they still don't involve Reginald, though I briefly considered his offer for this weekend. Even if it's football, it could fill the time I usually reserve for thinking about Marco, and might even lead to a date for my birthday. But I ended up texting Reginald that while I appreciated the offer, it's still too soon after my breakup with Marco. Besides, if I can't spend my birthday with the boy I really want, spending it with a boy I barely know won't make it any better.

During lunch break, I had texted Michelle that we needed to talk. She agreed, but only after I offered a bribe, which I'm holding now as I ring her doorbell. When Michelle opens her door, she takes the box of cupcakes from my hands without so much as a hello, like a sugar fiend in need of a fix.

"Oh my God, I love these things. I didn't know you went

to school near this place. My mom took me shopping at that mall over there and we had these cupcakes on a splurge. It's kind of crazy to buy a single cupcake for the price you could make two dozen at home, but these things are incredible."

I let her get all of that out before I tell her why I'm here.

"So the reason I wanted to talk to you—"

"I need milk. Wait—you don't want one, do you? Because you only brought four."

"No, they're all for you," I say, following her to the kitchen.

She's a little ungrateful considering I spent most of my pizza money on those cupcakes. She doesn't need to know I originally bought a half dozen for her, but ate two on the bus home, sneaking bites behind my Western Civ notebook since it's against the rules to eat on the bus. Now that I'm watching her pour a glass of milk, I'm wishing I'd showed some restraint and waited to have mine with milk, too.

"These are so effing good," Michelle says. Sometimes Michelle can curse like a sailor—well, if she actually used curse words, which she doesn't, out of respect for her preacher father. "So what do you want? Must be something good to bring me these."

"You know I'm friends with MJ Cooper. Well, I—"

"Really?" Michelle says, interrupting me between bites of the red velvet cupcake. "I thought y'all didn't hang out anymore. Any time I see her and you in the same place, seems like she makes a point of avoiding you. Except at that fire. Y'all were having a good ol' conversation then."

"Yeah, well, we had some issues, but those are all worked out and now I'm worried about her because—"

"You ought to be worried from what I hear," Michelle says. I guess I was wrong about those cupcakes keeping her focused.

"What do you mean?"

"Just that she likes to keep to herself and you can't stay out of people's business."

"Look, Michelle, what did you expect me to do about that whole Donnell situation?"

"Oh, I'm over Donnell, waaay over," she says, looking at me like she has a secret she's dying to tell. I oblige.

"I was on my way over to your house last night about six o'clock when I saw you and a couple of guys on your porch. Is one those dudes the reason you're way over Donnell?"

"You know Cisco, right? Of course you do—you got frickin' round-the-clock surveillance on everyone on Aurora Avenue you think is a criminal."

"Well, my surveillance game must be weak because I never heard of Cisco until Tasha mentioned him."

"Why would Tasha be mentioning Cisco?" Michelle demands, her voice going up a few octaves like it always does when she gets excited, which is why Tasha and I sometimes call her Squeak.

"I asked her about the latest gossip and she told me you were talking to somebody named Cisco, like I'm supposed to know who that is."

"Oh, okay," she says, appeased.

"So what's his story?

"Why should I tell you? These cupcakes are good," Michelle says, licking frosting off her fingers, "but they aren't that good."

"Seems like you might be really interested in this guy. It would be too bad if your father found out about your new crush before you even have a first date."

"Chanti, you wouldn't."

"You're right—I wouldn't, if you could just give me a little harmless information."

Michelle looks like she's considering shoving that cupcake in my face.

"I'm afraid to say. You might turn him into the police."

"If you want to run with criminals, that's your business."

"Donnell was my business, and now he's in jail."

"Donnell was trying to set me and my boyfriend up for a crime we didn't commit—and oh, yeah—*kill* me."

"That's true, I suppose, although it's your word against his."

"Girl, please. I'm not interested in Cisco. I was wondering about the other guy I saw on your porch last night. Is he Cisco's new second?"

"Really? He didn't seem like your type, although I've never seen you with a boy so I have no idea what your type is."

"Anyway . . ."

"He was just some random dude who asked Cisco for some directions and left like a minute later."

I suppose that's possible. The minute I recognized that hoodie, I went back inside the house because I didn't want him to think I was checking him out. Right now I'm working on the assumption Lux saw me the day of the fire, and that he was the random dude on Michelle's porch last night even though I never saw his face. That jacket just keeps appearing too many times for it not to have been worn by Lux every time I've seen it. But Michelle's explanation of why Lux was there is pretty lame. He couldn't ask his alleged girl-friend—the one who lives right across the street—for direc-tions? Michelle could be lying, but I doubt it since I can't imagine what she'd have to gain from it.

"Do you know where he was trying to get directions to?"

"No, I never heard that part. He just came up to the porch and said to Cisco, 'Hey, man, I'm lost. Can you give me some directions?' Like that."

"Just walked right up there to Cisco, almost like he knew him? Seems kind of dangerous to step to a gangster like that, especially after dark."

"That's true, but like I said, he was just some random guy. He didn't know Cisco."

I don't buy that, but keep it to myself. "What did Cisco do?"

"He didn't just give the guy directions, he walked him all the way to Center Street to make sure he knew where he was going and didn't get lost again. See? I told you Cisco was a nice guy. You just need to give him a chance."

Yeah, I might just do that.

Chapter 13

I love Saturday mornings, especially when they kick off a weeklong break from school and I wake up to the smell of pancakes and bacon, one of the few dishes Lana can't mess up. All she has to do is put the bacon on a microwave plate and pour pre-mixed batter on a hot skillet, so it always turns out right. Saturday and the smell of breakfast cooking also means she isn't dodging me this morning, and maybe now I can get some answers out of her. When I go downstairs to the kitchen, I find my assumption is wrong. Lana is pouring bacon drippings into the grease can, and instead of wearing her robe, she's dressed for work. Her weapons are on the counter next to her keys and cell phone. So much for getting her to talk this morning.

"Working on a Saturday?"

She takes a seat at the kitchen table so she can strap a holster and gun to her left ankle. "I offered to take a weekend surveillance detail for a friend. With Christmas coming next month, I could use the extra money."

I don't say anything while I get a plate from the cabinet.

"You're the only one I spend on at Christmas," Lana says in a fake cheery tone, "so all my time and a half will go to you. I know you've been wanting me to buy you a—"

"The only thing I really want you to do is stop avoiding me and do what you promised to do two weeks ago."

"I haven't been avoiding you. It's just so busy at work....."

"Mom, I haven't seen you in two days and we live in the same house. Even when your caseload is mad heavy, we've never gone two days without seeing each other. Even on your sixteen-hour days, you usually wake me in the morning before you leave and make sure you get home before I go to sleep. I don't need to be a detective to figure out you're avoiding me."

"Okay, you're right. You're right," she says a second time, like she's trying to convince herself. "Tonight—we'll talk over dinner. I'll make us something nice and we'll talk. I promise," she says before she puts her other holster and gun in her purse, grabs her keys and phone, and leaves me to eat breakfast alone.

Getting all feisty with Lana must have given me a little bit of courage because now I'm on my way to Center Street in hopes of finding Cisco, but first I make a stop at MJ's house. This isn't a social visit, and in fact, I'm hoping no one in the Cooper household finds me creeping around their property. I'm surprised the gate to the backyard is unlocked given what happened last weekend, until I remember that both MJ and Big Mama still believe MJ caused the fire. Even the fire report blamed it on the fireplace embers, but I'm not convinced.

I don't know what I hope to find, but from what I can tell, the back porch still looks the same as it did when the firefighters left. Lucky for me, they haven't called in a cleanup crew or a construction team yet. Even the ash can with the culprit embers is still on the porch, wood chips floating in the water used to put out the fire. No clues there. I scan the porch, the door leading to the kitchen, the walls. No clues anywhere. I'm about to go into the yard to see if the arsonist may have dropped anything on his way in and out of the yard when a breeze picks up a familiar scent. I sniff my shirt, then my hands, checking for evidence of my breakfast, but the smell of bacon isn't coming off me. It's coming from the house, and that's my signal to get out of there before someone spots me from the kitchen window.

I'm sitting in a front booth at TasteeTreets while I stake out the bus stop in front of the restaurant. When I talked to Michelle yesterday, she let slip some of the places Cisco conducts his business. I learned that his favorite spot on Saturday was the bus stop outside Treets. It has a shelter and even though it's all Plexiglas and clear, the front view from the street is partially blocked by a row of newspaper boxes. From the back—the TasteeTreets view—the money and drug transfer is blocked by Cisco and his customer as they sit on the bench inside the shelter. Squad cars can't really see from the street, and as long as Cisco doesn't stay there too long—longer than one or two patrol rotations down Center, he looks like a guy waiting for his bus.

I've been nursing my temporary courage and a chocolate shake for a little over an hour when I notice the same squad car has driven down Center two times. Cisco must have noticed it too because he gets up and walks to the curb to check if his imaginary bus is coming. I polish off the last of my shake, now room temperature, and head out to the stop. When I get a good look at his face, the first thing I notice is he looks a little older than I expected. Donnell is my age and he used to be Cisco's boss, but Cisco looks to be in his late twenties. I guess he's one of those bad guys who never moves up in the game and never gets out, either.

"Cisco?"

"Yeah?" he says, looking me up and down, but not in the way guys usually look a girl up and down. He's doing it the way criminals do to anyone who approaches them, whether they're a thugged-out gangster or an almost-sixteen-year-old girl in jeans, Uggs, and a puffer coat. Lana has fooled more than a few criminals in the exact same outfit, especially since she doesn't look much more than twenty-five. He's trying to determine if I'm a threat.

"I'm not looking to buy—"

"Buy *what?*" he says, managing to sound defensive and nonchalant at the same time. "I don't know what the hell you talking about. I'm just trying to catch a bus."

"I'm not a cop, either."

"Wait a minute—I know you. Chick that live across the street from Michelle, right?"

"Right."

"So what do you want from me?" he says, pulling out a cigarette. I'm always surprised when people do that. It seems like hardly anyone still smokes—well, except for weed. If people weren't still smoking weed, Cisco wouldn't be pretending to catch a bus right now.

"Just to talk. Do you have to be somewhere? Because I can talk another time if you're busy." Suddenly, my courage has cooled almost as much as the temperature has since I began my stakeout. I guess the weatherman was right about a cold front moving in.

"Naw, you stand right there. The cops just parked up the street in front of the bodega. You talking to me makes it look more legit. Act like you're looking for the bus."

I play along, and step out to the curb to look for a bus that I know won't be here for another five minutes because I have the schedule memorized. When a boy my age walks up and follows me back into the shelter, Cisco gives him a look that makes him reconsider. Not only does he stand outside the shelter, he walks a good twelve feet down the sidewalk. I feel kind of bad for him since a strong wind is the reason that cold front has arrived so quickly. But I guess he'd rather deal with the weather than with Cisco.

"Your girl Michelle send you to talk to me? She been pressing me hard and I ain't interested in doing time for messing with a minor. Tell her that for me, will you?"

"So why were you at her house last night?" Oops. Didn't mean to get pushy with a guy I'm certain is carrying under his own puffer coat. Let me just tone that down a notch. "I mean, I was on my way to visit her last night when I saw you on her porch."

Cisco looks over my head at the patrol car, and I know enough not to turn around. I'm hoping he'll help me since I'm helping him. Then he looks at me again, probably trying to figure out how much he should say.

"She used to be my boss's girl. My *ex*-boss. Told him I'd check on her from time to time. I don't know why—ain't like he getting out anytime soon."

I ignore the creepy smile he gives me, like we're in on something together. I mean, I'll stand here and give Cisco cover from the cops, but after today, I want nothing to do with him.

"What about that other guy who was there? Does he. . . is he one of your employees?"

"Dude was new to Denver, says he knew my old boss, thought maybe I could connect him to some people."

I'm really surprised how willing Cisco is to talk to me. I must give great cover.

"So you're going to help him out?"

"Hell naw. These medical marijuana joints opening up on every other block already cut into my business as it is. I told that mofo he won't be getting connected anywhere within a five-block radius of this block, and if he was smart, he'd get on the next flight back to California. Or at least stay the hell off my route."

California, where MJ's from and where the Down Homes are based. Coincidence, not so much.

"The cops gone yet?" I ask Cisco, ready to find MJ and stop being his impromptu accessory. "The bus really will be here soon."

"Cops left a minute ago," Cisco says, doing that creepy smile again. "Figured I owed you a little something."

"Why would you owe me anything?"

"'Cause you the reason Donnell ain't my boss anymore."

Great. Now I have a friend in the crime business.

"That isn't really the reason I helped take down Donnell. Maybe you heard about how he was trying to kill me and everything?"

"Don't matter the reason. Thanks to you, I run this now."

Then Cisco steps into a car that pulls up to the curb as if on cue, and he's gone.

Chapter 14

Lux must not have been scared off by Cisco's warning because when I get to MJ's house after my walk home from Treets, I find them coming out the front door together. MJ looks scared and I can't figure out what Lux looks like because he's wearing shades like he always does, apparently even when he's inside. I guess he's cool like that, but MJ has me wondering why she looks so nervous. This time, I don't think she's worried that I'll bust her to Lana or the cops for something, which is why even though we've been through a lot, she doesn't fully trust me. Yeah, I'm definitely not sold on her love triangle story between Eddie and Lux.

"Wassup?" is all MJ says, and she looks afraid just saying those few words to me. Unless cops with warrants are involved, MJ is never afraid.

"Just wanted to see what you were up to," I say, staring at Lux the whole time, trying to make out his eyes from behind the glasses, but I get nothing.

Lux's facial expression doesn't change—well, the part of his face I can see doesn't change—but MJ looks so stressed I'm worried she might puke.

"I gotta go," Lux says. "Remember what I said."

Before he walks down the steps past me, he pulls the hood of his jacket over his head and I notice a familiar tattoo on the back of his left hand. I might not be able see his eyes, but I know he's staring me down, probably something like that stare Cisco gave me a few minutes ago when I first walked up to him. MJ and I are quiet for nearly a minute while she watches Lux walk toward Center Street.

I'm wondering whether he parks on Center or doesn't have a car because he always seems to be walking. And now that I've heard Lux speak to MJ all threatening-like, I know for sure it isn't me that has her looking so worried. MJ and I don't share the same tastes in guys, and Eddie may not be the smartest dude on the block, but it seems crazy to creep around on a guy you clearly like—Eddie—with one that makes you look as sick and nervous as she looks right now.

"What was that about?" I finally ask because I'm beginning to think MJ is never going to speak. "Lovers' quarrel?"

She finally breaks her gaze from Lux. "What? Oh yeah, something like that."

"No, I'm guessing it's nothing like that."

"So why'd you ask?"

"Because I'm worried about you."

"Don't be," MJ says, heading back into her house, clearly not planning for me to follow.

"Wait, MJ. You're my friend. You saved my butt a bunch of times so now I'm returning the favor. Keep running around with your old gang members and you'll be back in jail. You're eighteen—no more juvie time."

"I know how old I am, don't need you to remind me. I told you, me and Lux together now. I didn't say nothing about him being in the Down Homes."

"You didn't have to. I know he's from California and new to town."

"Who you been talking to?" she says, coming back out onto the porch and closing the door behind her.

"It's cold out here. Can't we go inside and talk?" I ask, but MJ's silence means I'll be cold for a little while longer. "Look, I know he's got the letters DH on the back of that hoodie he seems to wear twenty-four-seven, and that it's brown—the Down Home gang's color."

MJ starts to say something but stops.

"I also know that tattoo on the back of his left hand is the exact same one on your upper left arm. Now I know why you never wear a sleeveless shirt, even on the hottest day of summer. But I saw it that time we had to go into the holding cell and the cops took your jacket. You had on a tank underneath and I saw it. It's your gang's mark."

"My *former* gang," MJ says, like that's the critical information here even if she's acting like a current member. "Just like it's Lux's *former* gang. So I know him from the old days. That don't mean we plan on robbing banks or selling dope together. Like I said, we just *together*."

"Yeah, about that. Eddie didn't seem to think he's just a friend with benefits. If I didn't know any better, I'd say Eddie is in love with you." I hate to snitch on Eddie, but I need to see MJ's reaction to that, and even the toughest gangster girl is going to reveal her true self when she hears the guy she likes might be using the L word about her. MJ doesn't disappoint.

"Seriously? Did Eddie say that . . . that he, you know?" MJ asks.

"No, but I can tell. Just like I can tell you're not creeping on him with Lux."

For the second time, MJ looks like she wants to say something but doesn't, and instead sits on the plastic-made-to-look-like-wicker sofa on her porch. Big Mama's design tastes inside her house and out say Miami more than Denver. The sofa cushions are covered in palm trees and toucans. I take a seat next to MJ and lean back against a big blue parrot. Normally I'd go with the Lana method of interrogation: stay quiet until the perp gets so nervous wondering what you're thinking that he gives up what he knows. But MJ looks scared again, and like I said, she never looks scared. Whatever is going on between her and Lux, MJ must think it's far more dangerous to tell me about it than to leave me in the dark and risk me busting her to Lana for hanging out with known felons and gangsters. So I let her know that I know.

"Look, MJ—I know you really are trying to go straight and stay in line with your probation officer. I know you want to get your GED and make Big Mama proud she took a chance on you. And now I know how you really feel about Eddie."

"Yeah, so?"

"So I know Lux has got you scared about something. You gotta start talking or I might jump to some wrong conclusions."

"You threatening me?" she asks, but doesn't bother to face me like she usually does when she makes her own threats. She just keeps staring across the street at Ada Crawford's house.

"No, I'm trying to help you."

"Like I said—don't."

I pull the lighter out of my coat pocket and hold it up, smooth side out.

"I found this in the yard across the street. Thought it might be yours."

"That's a man's lighter. Why you think it might be mine? I don't even smoke."

I turn the lighter around to show the side with the raised design. The same design on Lux's left hand and MJ's left arm.

"You're right, MJ. I never thought it was your lighter."

We both sit quietly for a minute before I speak again. "MJ, what does Lux have on you?"

This time, she does turn to face me and looks like she might try protesting again, but I guess I asked the right question. Instead of looking threatening, she seems defeated, like she has no more fight left in her. She opens the front door and this time holds it wide for me. I follow her inside.

Chapter 15

The smell of smoke is still in the house, but not as heavy as I had expected. I'm dying to see what the kitchen looks like, whether I was right about how far the fire had spread and how close the damage got to the basement door. Mostly I just want to check out the downstairs because I'm certain whatever confession MJ is about to make has something to do with her recent obsession with said basement. But MJ doesn't invite me to the kitchen when she goes for something to drink, so I wait in the living room.

"What I'm about to tell you can't get back to your mother," MJ says when she returns, handing me a glass of something purple. I take a sip—grape Kool-Aid. I guess Eddie was right.

"But what if she can help?"

"Promise me, Chanti."

I do, at least that's what I tell her, but some promises have to be broken and I know this will probably be one of them.

"You were right about our gang tats and me knowing Lux when I was still in California. He's my old gang brother; he and my ex are real brothers."

"That's violating your probation," I say.

"You think I don't know that? Believe me, when Lux showed up here a couple of weeks ago, I told him to get the hell off my porch, that he was looking for trouble if he was looking for me."

Before a few minutes ago, I would have believed all this tough talk from MJ—the girl is seriously badass. But after seeing her looking so afraid of Lux just now, somehow I don't imagine that's how their initial conversation really went down, but I don't interrupt.

"Then he tells me unless I want to make my recent birthday my last, I'd better shut up and listen to what he had to say."

"He threatened to kill you?"

"In so many words. He already blames me for his brother having to serve twelve years for armed robbery, like that was my fault. Now Lux is saying I'm the reason our old gang leader got his third strike and a life sentence, and if I don't do exactly what he tells me, he'll tell Tragic everything."

"Tragic? That's the gang leader's name?"

"Yeah, and if he finds out I'm the snitch who put him in jail, Lux is right. I'll be dead before the week is out."

I'm shocked. MJ once came close to letting me get killed to avoid being a snitch, but at the last minute, saved me.

"MJ, I can't imagine you narcing on a guy you know would kill you if he found out. I'm guessing if dude's earned a name like Tragic, he's not one to mess with."

"You ain't never lied. But it must have happened. I ain't even sure when I did it or what I said or who I said it to, but Lux claims he has proof."

"Let's come back to that in a minute. So what's he making you do in return for your silence?"

"He brought a box over and told me to store it here—"

"In the basement?"

"Right. That's why I was stressing about the basement when the fire started."

Like she's stressing right this minute, pacing across the living room floor ever since she came back with the Kool-Aid.

"What's in the box?"

"He didn't tell me and I didn't ask. Must be something he don't want anyone to know about, including me."

"You didn't open it to find out?"

"Hell no," MJ says, giving me a threatening look. "And you won't be opening it, either."

"How's Lux gonna know we opened it?"

"He has the box sealed up in a way that he'll know. He says if I open it, I won't have to wait on retaliation from Tragic to see my last day on earth."

MJ looks tired after telling me all of this, and drains her glass, probably as an excuse to go get a refill so she can try to shake off the confession. This is some serious ish and I'm pretty sure I'll be talking to Lana about it eventually, but not before I get as much information as I can. By the time MJ returns, I've come up with a few questions.

"So the day of the fire, why was he looking so happy that his loot was about to go up in flames?"

"I was surprised as hell when you told me that—didn't make no sense. I really thought I started the fire when I put those embers out there."

"The fire *was* caused by the embers—I read the fire report," I say, before realizing I was outing myself that I'd been snooping around. "I was convinced he was an arsonist so I had Lana pull the report, but she doesn't know anything about Lux. She believed the story I gave her and then I promised to stop playing detective so believe me, I didn't tell her anything about my suspicions."

"That's good, except now I'm really messed up. I was beginning to think you were right about Lux starting it."

"Why?"

"Back in the day, Tragic had an insurance scam going. Yeah, that's right—the Down Homes weren't just about drug-dealing and drive-bys," MJ says, apparently reading the surprise on my face. "On the real, we didn't even do much of that stuff. Tragic was more into white-collar crimes, like insurance scams. Lux was his firestarter."

"You mean—"

"You got it right. Lux really is an arsonist, which is why I began to think you might also be right about him starting the fire. But now you're telling me it was the embers, even though I'm pretty sure they were cold. Lux even asked me if they were cold yet."

"Wait—he was here when you put them on the porch?"

"Yeah. He came by early to check on the box and I was in the middle of cleaning out the fireplace."

"Kinda early in the morning for that."

"Before I had to leave for work at the bodega, I was trying to get through the list of chores Big Mama gave me to do before she got back to town."

"Lux saw you put the embers out there, which means he knew how to make it look like you started the fire accidentally. You didn't leave Lux here in the house when you left for the bodega, did you?"

"I ain't crazy. I wouldn't trust that snake in my grandmama's house. He left when I did."

"So he came back, started the fire and I caught him in the act. Well, a few minutes after the act."

"But the fire report said—"

"Yeah, and it also said the embers ignited a flammable substance. You didn't have bacon for breakfast this morning, did you?"

When I walked into the house, I smelled smoke but no bacon, even though the scent was strong this morning when I was out on the back porch snooping around.

"No, we haven't used the kitchen since the fire. Been eating out. Why does that even matter?"

I head for the kitchen, where I take a quick look around. Every grandmother I know has a grease can; they view pan drippings as liquid gold when it comes to cooking. Even can't-cook Lana has one, a gift from my own grandma.

"Where's Big Mama's grease can?"

"I know you ain't about to cook when I need help figuring out this Lux situation."

"No, I'm just trying to confirm something. Go with me for a minute."

"All right. It's usually on that counter right there."

"You mean the empty counter?"

MJ goes to the fridge and starts looking through all the shelves. "Sometimes she keeps it in here, but I don't see it."

"Because Lux took it that morning. That's the flammable substance the fire report is talking about. Your back porch smells like bacon grease even though y'all haven't cooked since Sunday."

"Why grease? Wouldn't he just use gasoline like every other firestarter?"

"Ever seen a grease fire? Lux is good. He set fire to the kitchen wall, same wall that has the gas oven on it and the counter where the bacon grease sits. Firemen would notice the smell of gasoline, but the smell of bacon makes sense. If they even noticed it."

"But how we know for sure it was Lux?"

"He didn't realize it was me, or I don't think he did, but he sat next to me in the bus shelter a couple of days ago and he must not have washed his hoodie because it reeked of smoke and bacon. At the time, I thought the scent was coming from Treets. But now I know better."

MJ still looks a little skeptical.

"Then there's the lighter. You and Lux are the only Down Home gang members on this street as far as I know."

"Excuse you. *Former* members."

"Anyway, I found the lighter in Ada Crawford's yard right where he was standing that morning, jiggling his hands in his pocket like he was nervous or cold. The lighter probably fell out then."

"Before he left a few minutes ago, Lux did ask if I'd found anything in the house or around the yard that didn't belong, but he wouldn't say what it was," MJ says, looking at me and nodding.

"Our first instincts were right. The embers were probably cold when you put them out, but he added some fresh wood chips to the ash can, put down the bacon fat, and lit a fire. He was an arsonist for an insurance scammer. He knows how to make a fire report look the way he wants it to look. The question now is why."

"That's what I don't get. He comes over here every other day to check on the box to make sure I haven't opened it, and whatever is in there must be something big if he brought it all the way here from California to hide."

"It's got to be some kind of evidence," I say, "something that will incriminate him either to the cops or to the Down Homes. That's probably why he's back in Denver—had to get out of L.A. and didn't feel safe leaving the box there."

"So why not get rid of whatever it is in the first place? Why bring it to me to hide?"

"It must have some kind of value for him, enough to make him risk holding on to it. But now something's changed for him, making it more dangerous for him to hold on to whatever it is."

"And he has to burn down Big Mama's house just to get rid of it? Why not just take the box and throw it in Cherry Creek reservoir or burn it out in a field somewhere?"

"Good question. Maybe someone's watching him. He knows it and he can't risk being seen taking the box out of the house."

"Damn, Chanti—if you right, I'm in hella trouble. That means Tragic already got eyes on me."

Chapter 16

For hours, MJ and I brainstormed how to free her from this situation, but we came up empty. At least that's what I told MJ. I have a few ideas brewing, but I won't know which way to go without getting a look at what's inside that box. Until I manage that, all I can do is leave MJ with the promise that I'll think of something. She also made me swear I wouldn't tell Lana—and I don't plan to, at least not yet. I need some hard facts and a few solid theories before I talk to Lana. Right now I need to focus on the talk she promised we'd have at dinner tonight.

I don't want to give Lana any excuse to blow me off, so I make sure dinner is ready to go when she gets home. There's a rotisserie chicken from Safeway keeping warm in the oven, a bagged salad kit in the fridge, and some potatoes cleaned and ready to pop in the microwave. I even made cupcakes from a box mix. That's my version of a gourmet meal, and it's still tastier than just about anything Lana cooks. I also spent a couple of hours cleaning the house top to bottom, grateful for the time to burn off my MJ worry because I don't want Lana suspecting anything about anything or else I'll never hear the truth about my SD. Okay, *my father.* I guess if I'm about to finally learn the real story, warts and all, I'd better get used to saying that. I can't very well call him Sperm Donor when Lana finally answers one of his phone calls.

While I wait for Lana to get home, I want to read the fire report in full just in case I missed any other clues, but it isn't where I left it yesterday. I brave Lana's disaster area of an office and look for the manila folder that had the fire report, but there are about fifty folders all over her desk, the floor, pretty much any flat surface. I don't want to be all in her business, but I really want to read that report, so I look through a few folders figuring the fire report is probably on top of one of the piles. I've flipped through a few boring case folders when I land on one with my name on the papers inside.

It's the kind of stuff parents keep but you completely forget about, like my little handprints pressed onto construction paper in purple paint, and a blue ribbon from my third-grade science fair. Then I find my birth certificate, which I don't remember ever seeing. I read through the boxes on the form and learn I was born late at night. But it's the father's name box that makes me stop. *Unknown.*

Unknown? How is that possible? I mean, clearly my mother was no prude when she was my age, but how can she not know who my father is?

Just then I hear her keys in the front door. I put the birth certificate into the folder, take it into the kitchen, and stick it between two cookbooks.

"Wow, Chanti, the place looks great and . . . what smells so good? I was planning to cook for you."

"There's a chicken in the oven and I just put some potatoes in the mic," I say, trying my best to sound like I'm not about to snap. "So we can get right to eating, starting with the salad."

"Can I get out of my street clothes first?" Lana asks, but doesn't wait for an answer. I would have said, *No, let's talk now.*

As she walks down the hall to her room, she asks me to

open the bottle of wine she keeps in the fridge. This is going to be serious. Lana isn't much of a drinker, but she keeps a just-in-case bottle of white wine cold for when there's something to celebrate, she's having a really bad day, or a friend is coming over for dinner. Considering this bottle has been in the fridge a few months, and in that time we've been through some serious stuff, this conversation is going to be rough.

"So . . . maybe we should talk before dinner," Lana says when she gets back to the kitchen. She drains the wineglass before we even sit at the table. "Okay, here it is. The reason I never mention your father, didn't want us to have anything to do with him, is because the last time I saw him, he was being arrested."

It takes a second for it to sink in that the only thing that kept me from having a father all this time was an arrest record.

"That's it—he was arrested? *I've* been arrested. I mean, unless the charge was murder or something terrible."

"It was for B and E."

"*I* was arrested for breaking and entering. That's nothing—not enough to keep me away from him."

"There was more to it than that."

"Like what?"

"Like he was guilty and you weren't."

"You don't know that for sure. He could have been set up just like I was."

"He wasn't. Like I said—the last time I saw him he was being arrested."

"Wait a minute—you were there?"

"I was . . . after the fact."

"So you didn't actually see him do it, whatever *it* is."

"Chanti, he did it."

"So what if he was guilty? Y'all were just kids. B and E for a minor is like, what—a year sentence, tops? I wouldn't even have been walking by the time he got out of jail. Look at MJ. Serving time doesn't mean you're bad forever. He could have gotten himself straight and . . ."

It occurs to me that even if he did go to jail, he's been out a long time and hasn't looked me up or anything. But since Lana's the one who's here, she gets my anger.

Lana gets up to refill her wineglass, then rejoins me at the table. So there's more.

"Why didn't he ever try to see me?"

"That's the part I've been afraid to tell you, Chanti. His going to jail became the least of it over time, and I just missed the right time to tell you and then I couldn't figure out how to make it right—"

"You're rambling, Mom. Just tell me."

"He . . . your father doesn't know about you."

"Doesn't know *what* about me."

"Anything. I never told him I was pregnant."

What? Is she kidding me?

"But you said you told him and he didn't want any part of having a baby. You said it worked out for the best that he ditched us."

"I know. It wasn't just the B and E or the jail time. He really *was* bad news. I never lied about that. It was just best we didn't—"

"Stop. Just stop. Let me think for a minute."

I get up from the table and start pacing around the kitchen, trying to make sense of her words. Lana just watches me, waiting. She isn't telling me something. There's more to it than a B and E. There has to be.

"What aren't you telling me? What does 'bad news' mean, anyway? You're always saying that, but it tells me nothing. And would you even tell me the truth, anyway?" I say, pulling the folder from between the cookbooks and placing the birth certificate on the table in front of her. "It says my father is un-known. Is that true, or is everything you've told me so far a lie?"

"Of course I know who your father is. That . . . it was just easier to do it this way."

"I wasn't even born yet when you decided I didn't need to know my father. I was just a plus sign on a pregnancy test stick. How do you get to decide that?"

"Chanti—"

"You know what? Forget it. You're just going to tell me more lies, anyway. I hope you enjoy your dinner."

I leave her at the table, grab my bag and coat, and ignore her when she asks where I'm going as I slam the front door behind me. She's super cop. She'll figure it out.

I couldn't have told her where I was going anyway, because I have no idea. I only know I can't be within talking—or screaming—distance of my mother right now. I start by going across the street to Tasha's, only to have her dad tell me she's working at the movie theater tonight. I even go two doors down to Michelle's place, but her mom tells me she's on a date. Of course she is—it's Saturday night. Michelle would never be home, dateless, on a Saturday night. There's MJ, but she's got her own problems to deal with, so I just sit in Lana's car, parked in front of the house.

I know Lana watched me the whole time I was walking up and down Aurora Ave looking for someone to talk to, and that she's watching me now. The blinds on the front window close shut and a second later she steps onto the porch. I swear to God if she comes out here I'm running down to Center Street to catch the first bus that shows up. She must know I'm thinking something along those lines because she only gets as far as the top step before she turns and goes back into the house. I guess she'd rather me freeze in the car where she can see me than be somewhere else.

I surprise myself when I grab my phone from my bag. "Hello?"

When I hear Marco's voice, I feel better before he even says another word.

"Do you have a second?"

"Yeah, what's going on? You sound—"

"It's my mom. She's making me crazy right now."

"Tell me."

And I do. I tell him about the conversation with my mom and the phone calls from my father who never knew I existed and everything that is making my life suck right now. The minute I finish, I wish I can take it all back. He already thinks I'm a drama queen; this will just confirm it.

"Better?" he asks. That's a good sign. He's still there—didn't hang up on the crazy girl.

"Yeah, better."

"Where are you?"

"In front of my house, sitting in my mom's car. I can't go back in there yet."

"Isn't it cold in the car?"

"No. Lana has all her surveil—I mean, she has a bunch of blankets and stuff in here. You know, winter driving preparedness and all that. I'm okay. Can we just talk for a few minutes?"

"We can talk for as long as you need. I can come there if you want."

"That's okay. Just talking to you is enough."

And it is—for nearly an hour, until his call waiting beeps.

"Damn," Marco says. "I forgot about her."

"Who? Oh no, did I keep you from something?"

"It's just um . . . well, I was going to see a movie with, um . . . Angelique and I was supposed to pick her up twenty minutes ago. Let me just tell her I can't make it."

"No, you should go. I'm fine now, really. You'd better go or you'll miss her call."

"That's okay. I'll call her right back."

Angelique interrupts one more time with the last call-waiting beep, and we're both quiet for a second. I almost wish he'd clicked over. How do you gracefully end a call that started with you ranting about your mother?

"You sure I won't be reading about you and your mom in the news tomorrow?" Of course Marco knows what to say, and even manages to make me laugh.

"I'm not as mad at her as I was an hour ago, thanks to you. I'll be all right."

"Okay, but call me if you need to. I'll keep my phone on vibrate at the movie."

After we hang up, I sit in Lana's car a few more minutes, soaking in the crazy that is my life. First, I need to help out a friend who is being extorted and threatened by some seriously dangerous people. Next, the one person on the planet I thought I could trust with anything just told me she's been hiding the biggest lie I can think of—*for sixteen years.* Then I have the sweetest, most perfect conversation with Marco that, for at least an hour, convinced me I can deal with the big fat lie that made me hate Lana for the first time ever. And just as I thought it really will get better, I'm reminded that Marco is not mine to make it all better. I seriously hate call waiting.

Chapter 17

I'm still not ready to see Lana yet, so I walk over to see MJ, the only person I know whose problems are bigger than mine. If nothing else, it'll give me some perspective.

"Did you come up with some ideas on how to get rid of Lux?" MJ asks when she opens her door. The smell of something Italian greets me—maybe marinara sauce— reminding my stomach I never had a chance to eat the dinner I made.

"No, but we can do some more brainstorming. And maybe I can get some of whatever smells so good."

"I found some leftover lasagna in the freezer, but I ate it all. I thought you and your mother had some big dinner and talk planned."

"We did—well, we had the talk, but I didn't stick around for the dinner. That's why I'm here. My mother is tripping and I just can't be at home right now. Can I hang out here for a little while?"

"Yeah, no problem. But I have to run down to the bodega for a second. I forgot to sign my timecard for the week and I ain't trying to hold up my paycheck. I'll be back in a few."

MJ leaves me in her house alone, a sign she either feels sorry for me because of my parental drama or she trusts me more than I thought. I hope it's the first reason so I won't feel so bad about what I'm about to do, even if it's in MJ's best interests. First I peek out of her front door and watch MJ until she's almost made it to Center, and then I run to the basement. I figure I only have about five minutes, maybe more if Eddie is working tonight and MJ spends a few minutes talking to him, so I check my phone and allow myself four. If Big Mama's basement is anything like ours, I expect Lux's box to be hidden under mounds of clothes no one in the house ever plans to wear again, boxes full of books no one ever plans to read again, second grade art projects, and a bunch of other crap no one remembers putting down there.

But Big Mama is no Lana, who is the messiest person on the planet. This basement is organized. The few boxes down there are neatly sealed and clearly labeled, except for one in a corner that I find hidden behind some well-used suitcases that have probably been carried by a few generations of travelers. They're so old-fashioned they don't even have wheels on the bottom. The bag check tags are still wrapped around the handles of all three bags. They belong to MJ and have the Denver airport code on them—probably from the flight that moved her to Colorado and Big Mama's house after she got out of jail. The large box behind the suitcases is marked *MJ's Stuff* and isn't sealed at all. The box flaps are just folded into each other to stay closed.

I check my phone and see I have about two minutes left. This can't be the box. The one I'm looking for should be hermetically sealed with wires and a bomb attached to it considering how afraid MJ is of whatever booby trap Lux has rigged. Then I realize the handwriting on the box isn't MJ's. I've spent too many nights helping her with her GED homework not to recognize her handwriting. And it doesn't match the formal cursive handwriting on every other box in the basement, writing that must be Big Mama's. The only disguise this box is wearing is MJ's name, probably meant to keep her grandmother out. Seems like a pretty lame disguise.

Well, at least until I see what's in the box, which is not at all what I expected. After I memorize how the flaps are folded, I stretch the long sleeves of my tee into makeshift gloves to carefully open the box. I doubt Lux will be dusting for prints, but I'm being extra careful—MJ doesn't need any more trouble from Lux than she already has. I move as slowly as my ticking clock will allow because a lack of sealing tape on the outside doesn't mean Lux didn't put some kind of booby trap on the inside. He didn't though. I also don't find any drugs, cash, diamonds or any of the other things I'd expect to find in the secret loot of a gangster. It's a box full of movie DVDs.

I don't want to disturb the box, but I do look at the top three layers of the neatly stacked DVDs and find they're recent movies, big box office titles. Most still have the cellophane wrap on them, but a few don't. Careful not to leave prints, I open a couple of the unsealed cases to make sure there's nothing but a DVD inside and I'm surprised to find that's all there is. No slim packets of cocaine hidden under the disk, no secret codes written on slips of paper. This is what Lux was willing to burn down MJ's house to destroy? With a minute left on my timer, I carefully fold the box flaps closed the way I found them and run back upstairs.

I plop down on the sofa and turn on the TV just seconds before MJ comes through the front door.

"I brought back some tamales they had left over from yesterday's Freebie Friday. I know you love 'em."

"Thanks, MJ. As good as that sounds, I may be a little too stressed to eat right now, but I'll take the tamales home for later."

I'm starving, but realize I'm too worked up about my mother's big reveal and from sneaking into Lux's stash for anything to feel good in my stomach right now. I know I'll have to deal with my mother eventually, but I'd rather it be later than sooner, so while pretending to watch TV, I focus on MJ's problem instead. I'm thinking if Lux lied about rigging his box and had MJ afraid enough to leave it alone, he might also be lying about the dirt he has on her that he claims proves she set up Tragic. For that matter, it's always safe to assume that anything a crook says is a lie and work from there.

"Speaking of home, that's where you have to be at eight o'clock. Hope that's enough time for you and your mom to cool off."

"What happens at eight?"

"Lux is coming by to check on his box. It'd be best if you ain't here."

Wow. Glad I was careful to leave the box the same way I found it. Now that I know what's in the box, I'm really curious why Lux is all the time coming over to "check on" it. You'd think it was a live plant he had to water. Or at least a cache of drugs he had to periodically shoot up or sell.

"MJ, what evidence does Lux claim to have on you?" I ask as I follow her to the kitchen. "Photos, incriminating emails or texts that prove you set up Tragic? Have you actually seen any of the evidence?"

"No, because it isn't the kind of evidence you can see."

"So it's invisible evidence?"

This part of the mystery—whether Lux really has any proof MJ is a snitch—may be easier to solve than I expected.

"I may not be an Einstein like you, but I'm not stupid either," MJ says, reading me almost as well as Lana. "I had this friend in juvie. You know how it is—in there you need somebody you can trust to have your back."

"Yeah, I actually do know thanks to you," I say, recalling last summer when MJ's gang dealings got us both arrested.

"We weren't even in there four hours. And I had your back, right?"

True. MJ saved me from a serious butt-kicking, but it was also her fault I was there in the first place. I nod.

"Most people need a full crew, but together me and Mya were tough enough to take on just about any gang in there, so we didn't bother running with a whole gang like most people inside do."

I can believe that if Mya was as scary as MJ.

"Mya was fierce in a fight. I can handle myself in your basic street-fight technique, but this girl knew all that martial art crap, like karate and that Israeli army fighting thing, um . . ."

"Krav Maga," I offer to keep the story going.

"Yeah, that's it. She moved to the States from Israel when she was a kid, and her father had been in the military over there. He taught her to fight, or at least that was the story she gave me. But now I really know why she was so badass. She was a cop."

"You mean a former cop?" I ask, even though I know it doesn't make sense. No former cop is under eighteen, and even if she was and went bad before her eighteenth birthday, they wouldn't put her with the general inmates.

"No, she was in there undercover."

"I'll check with Lana, but I'm pretty sure cops don't go undercover into gen-pop prison, even in juvenile correction. That would be a death warrant, not to mention even the best undercover cop can't fool a building full of cons. One or two at a time on the street maybe, but not hundreds of them."

"Lana can't know about any of this, Chanti. You promised."

"Okay, okay. So she was in there investigating what exactly?"

"Lux never said what, but it all makes sense. He ain't lying about it."

MJ puts her plate of nuked tamales on the table next to a big glass of milk. That's a surprise. I'd expected MJ to pull out some illegally gained beer from the bodega since her boyfriend wouldn't card her. No, not beer—a forty ounce of malt liquor. I guess even friends can profile.

"So what did Lux tell you to convince you Mya was a cop even though up until his claim, you had trusted her with your life for two years?"

"He didn't have to tell me nothing, I figured it out myself once he pointed out a few coincidences. What the hell?" MJ says, putting down her fork.

"Huh?"

"The basement door is open."

Oh snap, Chanti.

"Barely. More liked cracked than open. So what?"

"So I know it wasn't open earlier today. I checked."

"That happens all the time in the winter. Big Mama does keep it pretty warm in here and you just came in from the cold."

"What's that got to do with the basement door being open?"

"Maybe it wasn't closed all the way, and then the convective air flow created when cold air followed you into this really warm house drew the basement door open a crack."

I guess science isn't really MJ's thing because she's looking at me like I'm speaking Urdu.

"Look, I don't know what all you just said, but that ain't what happened. Damn if I ain't ready to hurt somebody. I gotta eighty-six this game right now."

All right, it's finally here—the day MJ Cooper gets so tired of my snooping she gives me the beatdown that ends our friendship. I'm preparing to take a hit when MJ says, "Lux must be breaking into Big Mama's house when I'm gone. What if Big Mama was here? Uh-uh, I ain't having it." She grabs her coat off the hook near the back door.

"Wait a minute, MJ. Don't get all crazy," I say, glad she's ready to get all crazy on Lux instead of me. "Lux will be over here soon enough. Let's keep talking this out rationally so we can come up with a plan that doesn't involve you possibly getting killed."

"Ain't nobody dying in this here situation but Lux."

"I believe it, but let's just keep talking anyway."

MJ reluctantly puts her coat back on the hook and returns to her tamales and milk.

"Okay, so you were talking about these coincidences with Mya. Tell me some of them."

"Well, like I said, the girl was damn near lethal in a fight. She knew a lot about the law and was always asking questions."

"Except for that lethal-in-a-fight part, you just described me."

MJ doesn't look convinced. "She also followed all the rules and never got in trouble. She was like the guards' pet. They loved her."

"Just because she followed all the rules doesn't make her a cop. And they loved her because she was a model prisoner."

Now I can see the doubt starting to shade MJ's face.

"Did you ever tell Lux about Mya—I mean before he arrived with his box and started blackmailing you?"

"Cons always talk about friends and cellmates, ain't nothing strange about that. We traded stories last summer, that night when . . . I mean, yeah, I told him. So?"

"So you gave him all the information he needed to concoct this story that your prison BFF was really an undercover cop who betrayed your every secret about the Down Homes."

"Huh?" MJ says, now looking totally perplexed. It's true what she said about her not being Einstein, but she's also not stupid. MJ is, and has been since the day I met her, the most gullible ex-con who ever lived.

"I'll bet you everything Lux is storing in your basement that he's lying about Mya being a cop or you being a snitch. Tragic is in jail for the same reason most crooks are—he eventually got stupid and got caught. No offense."

MJ doesn't seem the least bit offended. She seems relieved. "You really think so?"

"I really do. I think he just ran that game on you to convince you to hide the box. He needed to put it somewhere safe and you provide the perfect storage unit. He trusts you because he can hold this alleged "dirt" over you, and your commitment to not violating parole means you won't be letting other Down Homies anywhere near it. Whatever is in that box must be either really valuable or really incriminating," I say, though I can't imagine how a box of DVDs could be either.

"That makes me feel a little better."

"We're going to figure this thing out. We're also going to catch Lux in his lie so he can leave you alone."

"Thanks, Chanti. Now I won't have to kill Lux for breaking into my grandmother's house."

Chapter 18

The next morning, I wake to a massive dose of sunshine when Lana comes into my room and opens the blinds. It must be long past seven o'clock for it to be that bright.

"I overslept," I say, barely coherent. "I'll be late for school."

"No school—it's Sunday."

"Oh yeah," I say, trying to get my bearings. Nothing like being startled awake to confuse the hell out of me. "Then why are you up so early?"

"I have to take my friend's surveillance shift again this morning. But I promised myself I would stop sneaking out of the house before you wake up."

Last night was my first good sleep in a while so at first, I have no idea what she's talking about. Then I remember The Talk last night, and how we haven't said a word to each other since. When I finally came home from MJ's house, Lana was in her office. I went straight to my room and closed the door, expecting sleep to take forever to come, but I barely remember my head hitting the pillow.

"Chanti, I know you must be really angry with me right now—I'm kind of angry at myself. But even after what I've told you, especially because of what I've told you, we have to stick by the agreement."

She's talking about the agreement we made about the same time my hormones started to kick in and we had our first real argument. She left for work angry at me and I was at home cursing her when her partner came to the house to tell me Lana had been in a traffic accident during a pursuit. He said we didn't have much time; I had to get to the hospital right away. It turned out okay and we did get more time. After that, we made a pact that no matter how angry we were, we couldn't part without promising that it would eventually be okay between us.

"Is it okay for me to leave?"

"Yeah, go." It's Lana/Chanti speak for I love you, which we both have a hard time saying. It's even harder this morning when I feel like Lana has sort of betrayed me.

"I should be home before dinner."

"Mom?" I call to her before she goes down the hall.

"Yes?"

"He should know about me."

She stands in the doorway and looks at me for a second, but leaves without saying whether she agrees or not.

I must have gone back to sleep after Lana left because it's close to ten o'clock and I never sleep that late. You'd think with all the crazy stuff going on with me right now, I'd be an insomniac. Maybe finding out my father didn't reject me unloaded a weight I didn't even know I was carrying.

After a quick shower and a bowl of cereal, I head down to the bodega to share with MJ some ideas I have about dealing with Lux. I'm feeling confident until I see Lux coming out of MJ's house carrying the box. The cold November morning apparently hasn't woken me up fully because I don't turn around and head back to my house before I'm spotted. That would have made more sense. Instead, I stand at the bottom of MJ's porch steps, foolishly thinking I'm going to get some kind of explanation of why Lux is coming out of the house when neither MJ or Big Mama are home. I know for a fact MJ is at work and Big Mama is still on one of her church missions. He looks at me but doesn't say a word.

"Hey, you left the door open," I say.

"So close it," he says as he walks down the stairs. The day of the fire, I noticed he had an odd gait as he walked down away from the crowd. Now I see that he has a limp, and favors his right side.

I follow him to his car. It looks new. Not to mention it's the first time I've ever seen him with one.

"Do you own a real coat? Because if you plan on staying in town, you ought to know we've got another four or five months of winter coming, no matter what the calendar says. This isn't California, and that hoodie won't cut it for a Colorado December."

"You don't need to know my itinerary."

"Just trying to be neighborly. Hey, I didn't think MJ and her grandmother were home."

"You win a prize," Lux says, putting the box in the trunk.

"What I mean is how did you get inside if no one is home? And why are you taking stuff out of their house?"

"Didn't MJ tell you I'm her man?"

"That's what she claims, but it still doesn't explain how you got inside. Big Mama keeps the house locked all the time."

"MJ gave me a key."

Considering MJ was threatening to kill him last night for breaking into her house, I'm pretty sure he's lying.

"I think . . ." I begin, trying to think of a way to suggest he's lying in a way that won't get me killed, but Lux interrupts me.

"I know about you, Chanti, and what *I* think is you need to stay out of other people's business," Lux says as he opens his car door. "Unless you want to get hurt."

Yeah, those are the right words. I shut up quick and apologize for bothering him. Before he drives off, I manage to get his photo using my phone, and another of his license plates. Well, not *his* car because it's a rental—there's a sticker on the bumper. I close the front door to MJ's house and then head for the bodega, where I find Eddie at the counter talking to a customer about her sore feet.

"Sorry to interrupt, Eddie, but I'm looking for MJ. It's really important. Is she in back?"

Eddie apologizes to the customer for my rudeness, then says, "MJ took the day off. She called me last night and asked if I'd take her shift this morning."

"She hasn't been in at all?"

"No, I haven't seen her since yesterday."

The customer figures out she's on her own and goes off down the center aisle in search of bunion pads.

"Really? Did she say why she couldn't come in?"

"No, and she also wouldn't tell me why she called off our date last night."

Well, that was probably because I was there most of the evening, followed by Lux at eight o'clock. She was too busy last night to fit in a date with Eddie.

"Probably stressing over her GED exams."

"I'm pretty sure keeping a date with me would have provided her some stress relief."

Eww. TMI.

"I was supposed to come by around nine after I closed the store, but she called a few minutes before that saying I couldn't come over, and that she wouldn't make it into work this morning, either. I'm starting to think something's up."

So am I. Oh snap. What if Lux checked the box last night

and could tell someone—like me—had looked through it? I can't imagine that's it because I was so careful not to leave any clues, but now my first thought is whether MJ is okay.

"I gotta go Eddie. If you hear from MJ, tell her to call me right away."

"What's going on, Chanti? Should I be worried?"

I lie and tell him no, but I'm beyond worried.

Chapter 19

I spend the next four hours at home blowing up MJ's phone with texts and voice messages, but she doesn't answer a single one. I'm just about to call Lana when I hear a knock on the door.

"Damn it, MJ," I say as I open the door, but it's Michelle, the last person I expected.

"Um, that's what the peephole is for," Michelle says, just walking into my house uninvited.

"Excuse you? Didn't your mother teach you some manners?"

"I *had* to Bogart my way in. It's the only way I was ever getting inside this house. You weren't going to ever invite me, am I right?"

I scan the house looking for any signs that Lana is a cop instead of a paralegal. She never keeps anything in plain sight—no *Police Monthly* magazines or boxes of bullets or anything—but I'm always a little paranoid. With Lana at work, there's no chance of a gun or holster on the coffee table. So I relax a little.

"I thought you were pissed with me so I never expected you'd want an invitation."

"I told you, girl, I'm over Donnell and I understand now that he was no good for me. Or for you. Especially for you."

"Really?" I say, surprised to hear Michelle being so rational.

"But this morning when I came out to get the paper for Daddy, I noticed you talking to that dude, the one that was asking Cisco for directions the other night."

Oh, so this visit is not social at all. Michelle is on a fact-finding mission.

"Yeah, so?"

"So I was wondering what you know about him. I mean, he can't be some random dude like I thought if Big Mama and them know him, and now you. Maybe he knows Cisco after all."

"Well, I don't know anything about him." At least not as much as I'd like to. And so far, I haven't connected him to Cisco other than that night he walked Lux to Center Street and gave him directions, which, after my conversation with Cisco, I'm guessing were directions for how to get the hell out of Cisco's territory.

"I guess I should ask MJ. She must know him if he's taking boxes into her house and—"

"You mean *out* of her house."

"No, in. Well, I mean both. I saw him take a box into her house, and a few minutes later he came back out with a box. That's when I saw y'all talking."

Okay, now I'm really confused. Why would Lux be moving the box back and forth? Did he need to add more DVDs from a stash in his trunk? But I got a peek into his trunk and there was nothing there; it was as clean and empty as any rental car trunk. And even if he did need to add something, why did he take the box with him when he left? Maybe I was right and he did suspect someone had been looking through them and decided MJ's basement was no longer a safe hiding place—for DVDs. I still have no theory on that.

I'm about to ask Michelle if Cisco has mentioned Lux since that night on her porch, but just then I get a text from MJ.

"Michelle, I gotta go, which means you gotta go."

"But I want to find out about—"

"I know, and the minute I have anything juicy to tell you about Cisco I will," I say, hustling Michelle out the door.

The last thing I need right now is Squeak chirping in my ear about Cisco. Once I see Michelle go back into her own house, I head for MJ's.

"Where've you been, MJ?" I ask once she lets me in. "I've been trying to find you all day."

"I can see that," she says, showing me her phone. "Eleven messages. What's got you so worked up?"

"Uh, maybe the fact that a scary dude is blackmailing you and now threatening me. Did you forget about all that since last night?"

"Threatening you?"

"Yeah, that's right. I was on my way to the bodega to find you when I catch Lux coming out of your house with the box."

MJ's expression goes from worried to angry in about three seconds.

"Lux broke into my grandmother's house? I told you that's why the basement door was open last night—he'd been in here."

I don't correct her—better Lux take the blame for that than me.

"I guess you were right. He was in here and took the box. Or brought it back and then took it out again."

"What?"

I'm about to explain what Michelle saw when the doorbell rings. I follow MJ to the door, which she opens to find a uniform cop and some other guy.

"Malone, what are you doing here?" MJ says. Apparently she knows the other guy.

"MJ, the police need to check your house. They received a tip you may be in violation of your parole."

Now I know who Malone is too—MJ's probation officer.

"You have a warrant?" I ask.

"Who is this?" Malone nods in my direction.

"My friend. Her mom—"

"Is a paralegal and I know you need a warrant for a search. An anonymous tip isn't enough for probable cause," I say, interrupting MJ. I know they're cops and everything, but undercovers don't even tell other cops unless they have to. Plus, no need playing the Lana card just yet.

"MJ—glad to see you're hanging with a better class of friends, even better that they know your Fourth Amendment rights."

"Yep, that's right," I say, trying to sound threatening, but probably not succeeding. "All those lawyers I hang around have taught me a little something."

"A *little* something being the operative word. They must not have told you neither a warrant nor probable cause is required for parolees," Malone says as he pushes past us and into the house. "Besides, who said the tip was anonymous?"

MJ tries to follow the officer when he leaves the living room to do the search, but her PO tells us both to wait here. I notice the cop left the room like he was on a mission, like he knew exactly where to go. MJ must be thinking the same thing because she gives me a questioning look. When we hear the hinges to the basement door creak open, I give her one. And when the cop returns to the living room in just a few minutes, not enough time for even a trained officer to finish conducting a search in a house he's never been in, we know exactly who called in that tip. But seriously, how much of a parole violation could a box of DVDs be? Unless they're stolen.

Just then another uniform comes through the front door and Malone stands up.

"What the hell is going on?" MJ says.

"Mary Jane Cooper," the first officer says and I barely notice hearing MJ's full name for the first time because I know exactly what he's about to say next, especially when the second officer asks her to assume the position. "You're under arrest for felony possession of a controlled substance, possession of a firearms by a felon, and violation of parole."

Now I know what was in the box Michelle saw Lux taking into the house.

Chapter 20

Not that I had to remind her, but before they put MJ in the squad car, I yelled to her not to say anything to the police until I could get her a lawyer, call Big Mama, and find Lana. Now I'm sitting with Lana at her desk at the police station, Big Mama is driving home from Grand Junction, where she was doing some of her church missionary work, and the lawyer has just arrived.

Lana stands up to greet him, and they do the European cheek-kiss thing, which would seem weird for my mother, especially while she's on the job, but I suspect they once had a thing when she worked at his law firm as a paralegal. When I was arrested for some burglaries a few months ago, Lana had to get his help and blow her cover. When she left his firm, she'd told him she had found a better-paying paralegal job, not that she was enrolling in police school. Now three people in Denver outside the department know my mother's a cop: me, MJ, and this lawyer who we seem to be keeping busy lately.

"Mr. Chatman, MJ didn't do this. I know it for sure and—"

"Hi, Chanti," he says, shaking my hand. "If you vouch for her, then I know she's innocent. But I'd better go talk to her first. I just wanted to let Lana know I was here. Does Mary Jane have any family here?"

"Don't call her Mary Jane. I don't think she'll like it much."

I haven't confirmed this, and never thought to ask her what MJ stood for, but seeing how she's never told me, I'm going to assume she doesn't like it. Besides, her full name *sooo* doesn't fit her.

"She's eighteen. You can talk to her without guardian consent," Lana says. "And believe me, this one knows her rights *and* her way around cops and lawyers."

"We're her family," I add, to soften Lana's totally unnecessary editorial on MJ's knowledge about the legal system. "At least until her grandmother gets here. She's three hours away, but she'll be here to post MJ's bail."

When Mr. Chatman leaves to find MJ, Lana asks me why I'm so certain she's innocent.

"Lana, you don't think those were her drugs and weapons, do you?"

"No, but I want to know why you're so certain they aren't. I can tell it isn't just vouching for a friend. What have you been up to?"

"I know I promised no more investigating, but this thing with MJ just kind of happened and—"

"Chanti, what do you know?"

I tell her everything I know so far, starting with the house fire and my suspicion Lux set it, and ending with what I saw in the box the day before Lux switched out the DVDs for drugs and weapons.

"What I don't get is if he was worried about being outed on his secret stash of DVDs, why not just take them and run?" I ask Lana. "Why did he have to set up MJ? For that matter, why are DVDs so important he'd ask MJ to hide them without telling them what they were, and turn around and try to destroy them?"

"Maybe they were stolen master copies, or uncut versions not meant for public sale. Lux and Tragic did operate out of Los Angeles; they may have had contacts in the film business. He probably intended to bootleg them at first."

"Bootleg DVDs aren't all that serious, are they?"

"Don't ever say that to the feds. That little FBI warning at the beginning of DVDs is no joke. We're talking millions of dollars in illegal business. When I was on assignment to the FBI, I learned they have a whole department just for cyber crimes. Bootleg DVDs keep them plenty busy."

"Okay, so it's serious."

"Maybe Lux didn't tell MJ what they were because he was afraid she'd steal them, make the bootlegs and sell them herself. If he's from her old gang, Lux knows a different MJ than the girl you and I know."

"I can see that. But what about the rest?"

"He could have gotten angry that MJ was questioning him. Maybe you're right and even though you didn't notice any boobytraps, maybe he could tell someone—you—had been in the box."

"What if MJ is in jail because of me?"

"If Lux is like every other con I know, taking MJ down was probably part of the plan all along, whether you opened that box or not."

"Why do you say that?"

Lana leans back in her chair and starts staring at the ceiling like there must be hidden clues up there, so I know she's thinking through the clues we actually have.

"It may be big business, but there's more to this than bootleg DVDs. You haven't talked to MJ about what went down when Lux came to visit her last night?"

"No, we didn't get a chance before the cops came to her house."

"She must know more about him than we think. She may not even be aware of it, but Lux wants to make sure she doesn't tell anyone what it is, or at the least, make her an unreliable witness. He either realized that last night and had to act, or he was planning it to go down this way all along."

"The theory I was working on before she got arrested is that Lux was the one who narced on Tragic. You know, blame someone else for your crime and divert suspicion from yourself."

"It's a good theory," Lana says, then smiles. But the smile fades quickly. Poor Lana is always stuck between being proud to have a kid who is a good detective and being pissed off that I'm always sleuthing and getting into some kind of trouble.

Chapter 21

I sleep in Monday morning, even though Lana came in to tell me she was leaving for work. Here it is, the official start of Thanksgiving break, and I'm actually wishing I had a class to go to. At least then I'd have a distraction. So I decide to just stay in bed a few hours longer, delaying the start of everything I don't want to deal with. Even my new dress, hanging on the back of my bedroom door, bums me out. I was so happy when I picked it out, imagining what it would be like the night I'd wear it. It's been longer than a minute since I had a reason to smile, but I do when I see Marco's number come up on my phone.

"I didn't read anything about a mother/daughter show-down in the paper yesterday, but I still wanted to make sure things were good with you."

"I'm fine . . . well, better than I was Saturday night. I'm really sorry—and a little embarrassed—about all that. I shouldn't have called out of the blue and dropped all my drama on you."

"I'm glad you did. You can always call me."

"I don't think your girlfriend would agree. Was she mad about you picking her up late for your date?"

"She knows you and I are friends. Friends help each other out sometimes, which is another reason I'm calling. I was thinking if you need cheering up, we could go to this Dashiell Hammett film festival playing downtown."

"Who?"

"Dashiell Hammett. He wrote detective novels that were made into films back in the day when movies were still in black and white. You know—Sam Spade, Nick and Nora? I figured you might like the film festival since you like cop shows."

"Not from the old days, I don't."

"That's when the directors had to rely on the writing and actors—no special effects and CGI. It was all about building suspense."

"I don't have anything against old movies. I've seen a bunch of them."

"Oh yeah?" Marco says, getting way too excited. "Do you have a favorite director?"

"Okay, I've seen maybe three old movies. But I do have a favorite—*Roman Holiday*."

"Is it a detective movie?"

"Some film buff you are. And not everything I like is about detective stuff."

"So tell me why you like it."

"This girl, she's a princess but not very happy about it so she escapes her fairy-tale life for a day. Because she spends it with the right guy, that ordinary day becomes the fairy tale. I don't know—kind of silly, right?"

"Seems perfect to me."

I can't help but wish this conversation was happening in person because who knows what would happen next. We'd probably break our agreement, that's what would happen next.

"You make watching ancient movies sound tempting, but there's still the problem of you having a girlfriend. If I were

Angelique, I might be okay with friends talking on the phone"—*not*—"but seeing a movie is a whole different thing."

"I told you, she knows how it is between us."

"Does she know we sort of went out? Or definitely kissed once?"

Only the best kiss ever, although that's probably beside the point. When Marco doesn't say something right away, I take him off the hot seat.

"I can't make it anyway, as much as I'd like to. For you, I'd spend the whole day watching ancient movies, but I have some major stuff going on right now."

"You always have major stuff going on."

"I know. My crazy life, right? My mom isn't even the crazy-making part, at least not right now."

"Well, the doctor is in."

"I don't think you want to hear about this particular problem. It's the reason you'll probably be taking Angelique to the film festival instead of me."

I immediately wish I hadn't said that. It sounds like I assume we'd be together if we didn't have to worry about me inadvertently getting his cousin deported and I know that isn't the only reason. Even if I had Marco, I'd still be worried about what I'm supposed to do with him.

"Probably not—she doesn't like any detective movies, ancient or new."

"Your parents must love her," I say, wishing I could take that back, too. Snarky always sounds bitter when it comes to broken relationships.

"Are you still trying to solve MJ's problems?"

"Busted."

"Okay, but since we're on school break and I won't see you for a week, will you at least call or text me once in a while so I know you aren't in trouble?"

Before I hang up, I promise him I will, another addition to my growing list of promises I probably won't keep.

★ ★ ★

I'm standing next to Big Mama's car waiting for MJ to come outside. When I texted her that we needed to talk, this is where she told me to meet her at three o'clock. It's five after, feels like five degrees below freezing, and I'm cursing MJ for making me wait because I didn't wear my big coat. I'm about to go ring her doorbell when she finally emerges from her warm—make that sauna-like since her grandmother keeps it like Death Valley in there—house. I wouldn't mind being in Death Valley right now, at least long enough to warm up.

"You're late," I greet her, "and why'd you make me wait out here, anyway?"

"I don't want to talk about all this Lux business in the house. Big Mama is hanging around all the time, scared to leave me alone and even more afraid for me to go out. But she let up when I told her I'm just getting something to eat with you. She thinks you're a good influence."

Funny how perspective changes everything. Marco's mom wouldn't let us date because she thinks I might get his cousin kicked out of the country and Marco killed. Or at least turn him into a delinquent. Big Mama won't let MJ out of the house unless it's with me because she thinks I can improve the life of her granddaughter—an actual delinquent.

A few minutes later, we pull into Sonic and park at one of the eat-in-your car booths.

"Uh, MJ? Do you realize how cold it is out here? We need to go inside."

"I don't want anyone hearing anything about Lux or Tragic or my case. You want to talk? We eat in the car. I'll keep it running."

"That's dangerous, and they'll probably make you turn it off. Nobody wants to inhale gas fumes while they eat."

"*I'm* dangerous, and I'll tell them to go to hell."

"Yeah, that's just what you need—the Sonic people calling the police on you."

I guess MJ is tired of arguing with me because she goes to the drive-through window and orders. After we get the food, she parks in the mall parking lot across the street and keeps the engine running.

"You happy now?" MJ asks, unwrapping her burger.

Her tone suggests she really doesn't care about my state of happiness. I know better than to say I'd be happier eating inside somewhere, so I just nod and draw on my chocolate shake. I know I've been complaining about the cold, but I can drink a chocolate shake in any weather conditions.

"Next time, feel free to come to my house. It's hovering-grandmother-free and it's warm."

"I'm not talking in any cop's house, even your mother's. And I'm not talking at my house even when Big Mama is gone. Lux probably bugged it."

"That seems unlikely."

"You don't know everything, Chanti."

"You're right, which is why we're here. I need you to tell me everything you know about Tragic's last arrest, the one that got him serious time."

MJ looks straight ahead and I can tell she's thinking about whether to answer. She hates talking about anything from her old gang life, especially anything that might come back to bite her. Or kill her, when you consider she'll be narcing on gang members.

I try to coax her along. "I'm not asking for entertainment purposes. I think the reason Lux set you up, why he's afraid of you, has something to do with Tragic's arrest. I think Lux is the real snitch, but he told Tragic it was you."

MJ looks at me like this idea had never occurred to her. "If you're right, Lux had better be scared of me."

"Let's figure out if I'm right."

"What do you need to know?" she asks before she polishes off the last bit of her second burger. MJ can go through a meal faster than any boy I know.

"Okay, so I know Tragic was thinking about starting a Down Homes operation in Denver and that he sent Lux here to scope it out, using Donnell as his Denver tour guide. Why Lux and not someone else from the gang? Was Lux his second man?"

"Hell, Lux ain't even a tenth man. Tragic sent him because Lux is from Denver originally. He did a year in JD when he was, like sixteen or seventeen. When he got out, he moved to L.A."

"Ha, that's funny," I say. "You and Lux did something like a juvenile delinquent exchange program—he went to California, you came to Denver."

"Ain't nothing about this situation funny, Chanti. Anyway, Tragic was liking the Denver idea and sent Lux out to do some scouting."

"What does a gang leader scout for? Number of available bad guys to recruit, potential customer base?" I say, hoping I don't sound amused because I sort of am. Not about MJ's situation because it's mad serious, but about how she makes the whole gang life sound like it's just another business, like a corporation or a sports team. Maybe it is.

"Something like that. He needed to know if there'd be competition from existing gangs, whether they'd be easy to take out or tough enough to leave alone. Will people in the neighborhoods he set up be able to afford his services? Can he use local distributors, should he relocate some of his own, or should he hire locals? Stuff like that."

Wow, it really does sound like a startup business, except I'm guessing the local distributors MJ is talking about are drug dealers, though I don't interrupt her to ask.

"Lux met with some locals to set up a meet for Tragic. If things went okay, Tragic was hoping to make a sale."

"Sell what?"

"I never knew that part, but whatever it was, only Tragic was there to sell it—to undercover cops, it turned out. At the last minute, Lux couldn't make it."

So Tragic was based in L.A., but was arrested here. Good to know—maybe I can use my sources to get more information about his arrest.

"That's real convenient for Lux. My Lux-as-the-real-snitch theory is starting to look good, huh?"

"Naw, Lux had a good reason to bail on Tragic. He was in the hospital emergency room."

"Did it have something to do with his left leg?" Lux could have been born with an odd gait, but I'm taking a guess.

"Yeah. How did you know?"

"I noticed he has a limp and favors his right side. So what happened—some kind of gangland turf war gone bad?"

"You watch too much TV, Chanti. Lux accidentally shot himself in the foot."

I had figured dude wasn't that bright, but I underestimated him. Being in the emergency room with a bullet in your foot is a pretty good alibi. I'm about to ask MJ some more questions when she gets a text. She reads it, then bangs her fist against the steering wheel.

"What is it, MJ?"

"Lux says he just told Tragic I was the one who set him up. That fool is going to make me hurt him."

Chapter 22

When MJ tears out of the mall parking lot, she doesn't go in the direction of Aurora Avenue, which I point out to her.

"That's because I need to visit someone first."

"Not Lux."

"Hell yeah, Lux."

"This is a really bad idea, MJ. For one, I gotta believe it violates the conditions of your bail. For two, Lux is kinda scary."

MJ looks over at me, a second too long considering the speed she's going, and says, "And I ain't?"

"Oh, no—you're really scary, especially right now when you're going sixty in a thirty-five, which I'm certain is another violation of your parole and bail."

That gets her to slow down, but she still keeps driving toward Lux's place, which I see now isn't too far from the mall because we're turning into an apartment complex. MJ pulls in front of one of the buildings, parking in a numbered space. When I open my door to get out, she tells me to wait here, but she can barely get out of the car before some woman runs up on her. I get out, too.

"Look, heffa, you're in my parking space again," the woman tells MJ. I don't know where this chick came from, but she must be like my neighbor Mrs. Jenkins, watching for people to park in her space just so she can run outside and go off on them. I don't think she just happened to be leaving her apartment when we arrived because she doesn't have a purse. According to Lana, the only women who don't carry some kind of bag are hookers and joggers, at least in her experience.

"It'll only be there for a second. My friend will move the car if you need the space," MJ says, throwing me the keys as she continues toward the apartment building.

The parking space chick blocks MJ's path. Oh, that isn't good.

"That's not the point. The point is that's my space and I told you the last time that if you did it again, I was calling the police."

"Excuse me, but the police wouldn't write a ticket for this, since you're on private property." Both MJ and the pissed-off woman look at me like it's their first time seeing me. "Um, I'm just saying . . ."

"I ain't got time for this. Get the hell out of my way," MJ says, shoving the woman. Okay, *now* the woman would have a reason to call the police since MJ's shove might be construed as assault. Time for me to do more than just cite the law.

"Hey now, MJ. This nice lady isn't who you're mad at," I say, stepping between them. I doubt the lady is all that nice given the teardrop tattoo under her right eye.

"Like hell. I'm mad at her too, now."

"Well, she isn't who you came to see. One issue at a time, right?"

"Yeah, you right. I need to stay focused so I can handle my business," she says, leaving me and the angry woman on the sidewalk.

I get in the driver's side of the car and back out of the woman's space while she watches, hands on her hips and looking like she wants to hurt somebody. But by the time I parallel park the car in the fire lane right behind her parking space, the woman is gone. She's like a spy in stealth mode with all the sneaking up on you and sneaking away. I get out of the car to see where she could possibly have gone in five seconds.

That's when I hear all the yelling. I look up to see MJ outside Lux's apartment door and from what I can tell, it's Lux doing all the hysterical yelling. Maybe he isn't as tough as I thought, although MJ has more than a few pounds and inches on him. Then she throws him up against the wall, her right forearm rammed up against his chest and dangerously close to his windpipe. That's my cue to get up there before she commits about twenty violations against her parole and her bail.

I reach Lux's door just in time to hear MJ tell Lux, "I'm gonna kill you." I drag her away before she can.

I'm surprised to find Lana in the kitchen when I get home. Hopefully she won't notice I'm still wound up from our visit to Lux's place. Even though I didn't actually fight anyone, I feel like I could have if anyone stepped to me. It's sort of the way I always want to fight someone whenever I leave a Jason Bourne movie. I feel like I'm a badass just from watching someone else be one.

"You're home early," I say.

"I'm not really home yet. I was in the neighborhood running down a suspect and figured I'd grab some lunch—ham sandwiches. Want me to make you one?"

Speaking of badass. I know Lana's been a cop for a long time, but it never stops sounding weird to have your mother say stuff like that—*I was chasing a murderer, then thought I'd grab a sandwich.* Although in this case, it probably wasn't a murderer. Homicide arrests always require a boatload of paperwork and she probably wouldn't be home until the middle of the night if she'd gotten a lead on a killer this morning.

"That's okay. MJ and I just came back from Sonic." No need to tell her what happened between the restaurant and home. "Kind of close to home to be making an arrest. What about your cover?"

"If I locate the guy, I'll have a uniform make the arrest. So how's MJ doing?"

"Um . . . she's dealing with it as best she can."

"It's been crazy this morning, but when I go back to the department, I'll see if there have been any new developments on her case."

I just hope any new developments don't include Lux charging MJ with assault, but I'm banking on the typical bad guy M.O.—that Lux has enough dirt to hide that he wouldn't willingly get the police involved in his life.

Lana finishes making her sandwich but doesn't bring it with her when she joins me at the kitchen table.

"Chanti, I really did hear what you said the other morning—that your father should know about you. You're completely right about that, and he will, just as soon as I've checked him out."

"What is it you have to check? You're hiding something else, because I know you aren't this worried about a sixteen-year-old B and E charge."

Lana stays quiet, which confirms my accusation, but I'm still in the dark.

"Okay, if you won't tell me that, I have another question about him, and it's pre-arrest so you should be able to tell me."

"What is it?"

"The few times you ever talked about him, you said it was just a one-time thing, that he was just someone you met at a spring break party and that you barely knew him."

"Right" is all she says, but I read more in the way her body language changes. The story isn't "right" at all.

"First off, that so isn't you—meeting a guy at a party, hook-ing up with him like that. Even before you became a cop and trusted no one, that just isn't you."

"I was a girl, not the person you know now. You're going to be a whole different person when you're my age. You'll see."

"No, I don't think so, but let's say I give you the benefit of the doubt. We assume he doesn't know I exist, or if he does know you have a kid, that he doesn't know I'm his."

"So?"

"So why is he is he trying to contact you? Why is he so persistent? I may not know much about boys, but I do know there probably isn't a guy on the planet who will track down some random girl he hooked up with at a party sixteen years ago. Most guys would have forgotten you the minute he told his boys about you the next day at school and began his search for the next hook-up."

"Right."

"Would you please stop saying *right* and tell me something real, like if he was just some guy, why were you there when he was arrested? Or did that happen the same night y'all made me? Because that must have been one helluva night," I say, not realizing my voice has gotten louder or that I'm growing as upset as I was when she first admitted my father doesn't know I exist.

"I did meet him at a party. That part wasn't a lie, and neither was the part about our being together for a short time. But it was for more than one night, and I fell hard for him. It was mutual."

"So what happened?"

"A couple of months after we met, I found out about you and I was going to tell him. Then he was arrested and I never got the chance. It wasn't like I was going to marry him. I was so young, I wanted to go to college. . . . Seeing him being put into a squad car just made it easier not to tell him."

"I thought you fell hard for him."

"I did, but by the time he was sentenced I realized I was just infatuated. I'm sure that's all it was for him, too."

"I want to know him, Mom. I want him to know me," I say before I leave her and go to my room. I have more questions, but none that Lana can answer, like why he's trying to contact us after all this time. To be honest, I didn't spend much time thinking of my father until he resurfaced, and when I did, I spent it angry at him for not giving a damn. Now that I know Lana never even told him about me, I'm not sure what to replace the anger with. So far, the only thing I've come up with is curiosity—nothing more or less than that. But at least I'm not mad at him anymore.

Chapter 23

My conversation with Lana yesterday gave me few answers, but she promised to discover what happened to my father after he went to jail. That gave me an idea of a way to get more information about Tragic's arrest than what MJ has been able to tell me, which is why I'm meeting Michelle in her driveway this morning. I find Tasha there instead, leaning against Michelle's father's car.

"What are you doing here?" I ask. "I mean, not that I'm not glad to see you. Just didn't expect you."

"Don't even. I know all about what you're up to and I'm going on this little field trip with you and Michelle—for guidance and moral support. I think it's crazy, but y'all need at least one sane person along for the ride."

"Whatever, but I hope Michelle isn't running late."

"Please. She's been talking about this trip since the minute she got off the phone with you yesterday and called to tell me about it. What I'm trying to figure out is what's in it for you."

I ignore Tasha's question posed in the form of a statement. "You wouldn't think she'd be all that excited, especially since she kept telling me how I'll owe her big for this. And can either of y'all keep quiet about anything?"

"Chanti, you know I can keep a secret as long as you *tell* me it's a secret," Tasha says, which is true, though I don't think I should have to start every conversation with her by saying what she can and can't repeat. "Now Michelle—that's another story. Don't ever tell her anything you don't want someone else to know, whether you warn her it's a secret or not."

"Okay, so where is she? I wanted to be on the road by ten."

"She forgot something and had to run back in the house."

We finally get on the road by ten, although we are still almost late getting there. Apparently Tasha really does think that a visit to the state penitentiary is an actual field trip because she makes Michelle stop twice during the two-hour drive, once for burgers and the second time for a dipped cone at Dairy Queen. I have to admit I am glad for the DQ stop. It's a cold day, but I won't ever turn down a Blizzard.

When we finally arrive in Cañon City, Michele reminds me for the hundredth time that I'll owe her.

"And this will take more than a box of cupcakes. I mean, I still want the cupcakes, but I'm gonna need more."

"All right, Michelle," I agree. "Just get me inside and we'll talk about payment later, okay?"

"So this is really *your* visit?" Tasha says to me. "You'd better tell me what's up, Chanti, or your mama's gonna hear about this little trip."

"I just need to talk to Donnell for a minute, that's all."

"You need to talk to the dude who planned to kill you?"

"Yeah, I, um . . . I need some closure so I can move past that. I still dream about him holding that gun on me," I say, hoping to really sell it so she'll leave me alone about it.

"Seeing the guy that held the gun on you will give you closure?" Tasha asks, clearly not buying.

"That's right. I saw it on *Dr. Phil.*"

Once we're in the visitors' area, Michelle takes us through the process like a pro. The guard at the desk even knows her by name and throws her some game and of course, she flirts back. I guess she didn't get over Donnell until recently because it's clear she's visited him before.

"How often do you come down here?" I ask when we all take a seat in the waiting area.

"I've been a few times."

"And your parents let you?" Tasha asks. "I can't see the reverend giving you the okay on none of this right here. What lie do you tell him to get the car?"

"Daddy trusts me, I don't need to lie. But it makes him feel better if I do, so he thinks I'm in Colorado Springs attending a one-day youth church camp. That way if he checks the odometer, it looks right. I learned that from Chanti."

"Both your mothers must be so proud," Tasha says.

We only have to wait a couple of minutes before Michelle's name is called, but she doesn't get up to join me.

"Aren't you going in there with me?"

"I told you, I'm over Donnell. No need to bring up ancient history. I did what you wanted and got you in, right?"

"Yeah, but he's going to be a little disappointed when I show up instead of you."

"All the more reason for me to stay right here with Tasha, especially after you give him this," she says, handing me an envelope.

"What is it?"

"A Dear Donnell letter. It's okay—the guards already inspected it. Give him that and buy me a box of cupcakes and we'll be even."

"You only agreed to this so I can break up with him for you?"

"And can you believe I almost left the letter in the house?"

"I don't think Donnell's going to be very helpful after he's been dumped."

"That's why you give it to him at the end," she says as I walk off like I'm about to become a prisoner, not visit one. "And don't be all day. I want to stop by the outlet mall on the way home."

I almost feel bad disappointing Donnell—he looks so happy and expectant when I see him through the window of the door to the visitors' room—except he once wanted to kill me so I get over it. His look goes from confusion to anger once he sees it's me and not Michelle. It makes me sorry the visiting room is just tables, chairs, and a few guards instead of those little rooms with bullet-proof glass separating prisoner from visitor and two telephones like you see on TV.

"What the hell you doing here?" Donnell asks.

"Um, Michelle says hi, but didn't really want to come in. She thought it was best if you both moved on," I say, forgetting Michelle's advice about saving that information for the end of the visit. Fear will make you forgetful.

"So she sent you instead? She gotta know you the last person I want to see."

"The feeling is mutual, Donnell. You were going to kill me, remember? And we used to play dodge ball together." Although that may explain why it always seemed he threw the ball harder at me than anyone else. Maybe he hated me then, too.

"Wasn't nobody gonna kill you."

"No, I remember exactly—you said I was expendable."

"Oh that. I was just talking," he says, like he'd been talking smack about beating me in a game of H-O-R-S-E, which we also used to play together back in the day before he became a felon. "I guess any visitor is better than none. What you want, anyway? I'm pretty sure this ain't a social call."

"I'm surprised you're here in fed lock-up already. That whole situation where you were 'just talking' about me being expendable was barely three months ago."

"I took a plea. I still got a five-year run, but it's hella better than eleven. I'll be twenty-three when I get out."

And hopefully I'll be in another time zone by then, but I keep that to myself. In fact, I don't say anything at all because even though we grew up together, we're not sitting across a playground picnic table from each other.

"Whatchu want, girl? I know you ain't here to check on my welfare."

"Right, okay. MJ is in trouble," I say, hoping he never suspected she was the one who told Lana he was after me. I watch his face closely and see no flash of anger in it.

"What's up with MJ?"

"She was arrested for drug and weapon possession."

"Damn. That's her probation right there."

"Yeah, except I think she was set up."

"By who?"

"Dude named Lux."

Donnell's expression changes to exactly what I was half-expecting when I mentioned MJ's name. Apparently Lux has also pissed off Donnell once or twice.

"What's that mofo doing back in town?"

"Extorting MJ, and now setting her up for a drug and weapons charge, for some reason. If you could answer a couple of questions, I might be able to help her."

"Chanti, you sound just like a cop. Still playing detective?"

"I just want to help my friend."

"All right. I like MJ, and I'll do whatever I can to get Lux a room here at the inn. Maybe we'll even get adjoining cells. Then I can give him a beatdown whenever I'm feeling bored, which is every damn day. I believe that snitch set me up, too. How else would the cops know to find me at that house?"

That would be MJ's doing, but Donnell never needs to know. Besides, who's to say Lux wouldn't have tried to set him up eventually? Seems like that might be Lux's thing. That and arson.

"Lux ain't to be trusted. MJ hooked me up with him this past summer. I introduced him to some local meth cooks. His boss had a meth operation going in L.A. and he wanted to branch out here. I was supposed get him connected to some buyers in Denver."

"Buyers of meth?"

"Lux never said specifically, could be meth, could be copper wire, you never know. Gangsters don't tend to specialize. If there's loot to be sold and a market for it, we—I mean *they*—find a way to sell it. So I set up this meet between Lux and some locals, but he didn't want me to go. I figured then he might do me some double-cross. Should have trusted my instincts. Afterward, Lux asks if I'm trying to set *him* up because he recognized one of the locals as a cop who arrested him when he was sixteen and still lived in Denver. Got him some time in JD."

"He remembered a cop from what . . . four or five years ago?"

"You never forget your arresting officer. Never know when you'll get a chance for payback. So like you said, it's been four or five years and I guess by the time the deal I set up went down, she was undercover—"

"She?"

"Yeah, Lux said it was lady cop. She was cute, easy to remember. Anyway, he comes up with this idea to take out his boss 'cause he wants to take over the Down Homes, and promises to give me the Denver operation they were starting up."

"So you were in on the setup of his boss," I say, not trying to remind Donnell that makes him a double-crosser, too, but to make sure I have the story straight. He takes offense anyway.

"Chanti, I'm a businessman. I had to seize the opportunity."

"I believe it, Donnell. So then what happened?"

"He never gave me any details, he just told me to find a reason not to go to meet with him and his boss."

"What's the boss's name?"

"I don't know, Chanti. That's serious, wanting me to give names and everything."

"If it's who I suspect, he's locked away in a federal prison."

"That won't stop him from hurting me."

"But I thought you *really* wanted to see Lux in here with you, to be a source of daily entertainment."

"Can't give a beatdown from the grave."

I take another approach. "Is his name Tragic?"

"I can neither confirm nor deny."

Good, we're talking about all the same people.

"Turns out Lux didn't go on the meet, either," Donnell continues. "Like I said, I didn't get the details, but I know for a fact whatever the boss expected to find when he opened that briefcase, it wasn't cop-killers."

"You mean the bullets, right?"

"Right, and he had plenty of them, too, enough to make the police think he was planning to sell them. Lux threw some drugs in there for extra measure, but that was just a waste of good drugs. Once Five-O saw the cop-killers, they tuned him up right there, before they took him in. Messed up his left eye so bad he can't see out of it no more. At least that's what I heard."

Yeah, I imagine finding a guy about to sell illegal cop-killers on the street is the kind of thing that will make even a by-the-book cop give a tune-up. That's a beatdown, to you and me.

"So you never knew what was supposed to be in the briefcase?" I asked, although I already know.

"Nah, never did. But later, when I got word what was actually in there, I was shocked."

"Why?"

"'Cause Tragic made it a point not to mess around with

weapons. He told me so when he asked me to start up his Denver operation. Get picked up for drugs and what not, you don't do a lot of time if you got a good lawyer. Weapons is a whole 'nother story. And cop-killers? No way did Tragic think those were in that case."

"So Lux got away with it."

"For a while, anyway. He went back to L.A. and tried to take over the Down Homes, telling the gang he knew all Tragic's expansion plans and how to carry them out, that he'd become the boss's right-hand man while they were working together in Denver."

"That was a pretty quick bonding experience," I say, remembering what MJ told me about Lux not even being a tenth man.

"Yeah, that's what the Down Homes eventually thought. Once they figured out they were being played, they made it so Lux had to get out of L.A. quick if he was concerned about his health."

The guard announces that visiting time is up, which is perfect timing. I won't have to figure out how to say bye to a guy I played with as a kid who is now a state-pen convict I hope never to see again.

Before Donnell is led away by the guard, I thank him for his help and hand him the letter I almost forgot I was holding. Donnell takes it from me. He must recognize her handwriting on the envelope because he doesn't ask me what it is, only says, "Tell Michelle she ain't right."

I promise him I will.

Chapter 24

When I get home from my field trip, the first thing I do is hit the shower. Leaving the prison, I felt the same as when I visit a hospital—who knows what I may have picked up in there. I'm still getting dressed when the doorbell rings, and by the time I hurriedly finish and rush to the door, I open it to find no one there, but a padded mailing envelope falls onto my feet. I look around for any sign of whoever must have propped the envelope against my front door, but Aurora Avenue is deserted. I pick up the package expecting it to be for Lana, but it's addressed to me.

It contains three DVDs of black-and-white movies, and not because the director was trying to be artistic. I'm pretty sure the director didn't have a choice, given the movie covers. From the clothes and hairstyles of the actors, I'd guess the movies are circa 1940. I've been begging Lana to subscribe to one of those DVD subscription services, but I don't think she finally gave in. For one thing, she always says nine hundred channels worth of cable is plenty (like there actually are nine hundred channels!). For another, unless Lana subscribed to the lowest-rent DVD service she could find, this envelope doesn't look very official. The label with my name and address is printed, but other than that, nothing about it says legit. And there's no postmark, so the mailman didn't deliver it.

I drop the envelope and DVDs on the floor about the time my paranoia kicks in and my mind runs through scenarios of anthrax and mail bombs. Every scenario involves Lux. It's just way too much coincidence that he's running a DVD scam and I receive a package of DVDs.

A few minutes later, the doorbell rings again. This time I don't plan to open it until I look through the peephole and when I do, I find Marco standing there. That surprises me more than when I found the mysterious envelope. Marco has never been to my house before. Thanks to Lana, we're not exactly in the white pages. I also don't remember ever telling him my exact address.

"It's my turn to just show up at your house," Marco says when I open the door. "I know you said you were doing all right when we last talked, but I wanted to make sure. In person."

"You're really sweet, Marco, but I shouldn't have laid all my family secrets on you. It was kind of heavy . . . the kind of thing you only confide in a—"

"Friend—it's the kind of thing you talk to a friend about, right? Besides, I told you all my family secrets first."

"Right," I agree, though I was going to say it was the kind of thing you only confide in a boyfriend. The other thing I wonder but don't mention is why it's okay for us to hang out as friends but not as boyfriend/girlfriend. Do his parents have specific guidelines for this whole *forbidden to see Chanti* plan? Does being "just friends" make him less afraid of my sleuthing causing his family trouble?

"I get it if you don't want to talk about it, but if you need to, call me."

"Thanks, Marco, I really do appreciate that."

"Since I'm here, you gonna let me in?"

I was so surprised to find Marco at my door, apparently I forgot all my home-training.

"Oh yeah, of course. It is kinda cold out there, huh?"

"Kinda," Marco says as he comes inside.

"I can get us some sodas, or something." I say, feeling nervous even though we both know everything is strictly platonic between us.

"You dropped your DVDs," Marco says, picking them up before I can warn him that they may be rigged with explosives or bioweaponry. Or not. "Hey, I thought you weren't into old movies. This is one of my favorite directors."

"Those aren't mine."

"The envelope has your name on them. Someone must think you like them."

"Yeah, maybe my grandparents sent them. They like those ancient films. I guess they're trying to get me into it," I say, hoping my explanation doesn't sound too lame. I figure it's best not to tell him I think they're a gift from the arsonist.

"Your grandparents have great taste. Hitchcock is my favorite."

"Is that another detective from those old movies like that film festival guy you told me about?"

"Wow, I guess these really aren't yours then. If I wasn't planning to go into engineering or computers, I'd probably go to film school and this guy is the reason," he says, holding up one of the DVD cases as though that's going to make me understand who Hitchcock is.

"Oh, I get it," I say, realizing I got it all wrong suspecting Lux sent the movies.

"Get what?"

"You dropped these off hoping they'd convince me old movies are as great as you say they are."

"What? I didn't drop these off."

"Yeah, you did, because I wasn't interested in seeing that

old detective film festival. Pretty clever how you made it all mysterious, dropping off an anonymous package. Now I *have* to watch them."

"I'm pretty sure you'll enjoy the movies, but I swear it wasn't me."

Just then, I get a text from Lana. Perfect timing. As much as I'm enjoying Marco's visit and his little game with the DVDs, I really want to start working on the information I got during my visit with Donnell.

"That's the ringtone for my mom. I have to check it."

Other people's moms call or text to check up on them. Lana does that, but she also checks in with me so I know she's okay, too. When you have a cop for a parent and they're on the street working, you never know if it might be the last time you get to talk to them. I always answer, especially since Lana's the only parent I have. Although I guess that isn't exactly true anymore.

"I'm sorry, Marco. I've been a slacker host," I say, reading Lana's text, "but it isn't the best time. Can I call you later?"

"No worries. Let me know if you change your mind about catching that film festival."

Lana doesn't really have anything major to text me after all, just that she's on her way home and why don't we go out for dinner tonight. It's bad when you start looking for ulterior motives from your mother, but that's exactly what I've been doing since she told me it was my father she's been hiding from. I suspect that's what this dinner offer is about since we don't eat out very often unless we can pick it up from a counter and pay a uniformed cashier for it. Otherwise it's pretty much Red Lobster on her birthday and The Cheesecake Factory on mine, and maybe T.G.I. Friday's when I get a good report card, which is every semester.

That's where we are now because I wasn't creative enough to pick a special place to have another Big Important Talk about my long-lost father. Or not have one. I think I'm ready to hear the next part of my father's mystery, but I doubt Lana's going to tell me anything about the night he was arrested. That doesn't keep me from asking about it once we've given the waiter our order.

Instead of looking directly at her, I stare at all the buttons on the shirt of the waiter taking an order at the next table and hope he doesn't think I'm checking him out. Normally I like to read people when I question them, especially Lana, but I've learned from experience that this topic makes me a little crazy, and I don't want to go off in T.G.I. Friday's. Sort of like watching a solar eclipse—maybe if I don't look directly at her, I won't have a meltdown.

"So, any news on the paternal front?"

"No, but I'm working on it."

"He hasn't called in a while."

"Because I changed the number, remember?"

The waiter has finished taking the next table's order, so now I have to pretend I'm looking over the dessert menu.

"It wasn't like we gave him our old number, but he found it anyway."

"That's true, especially considering Mama and Dad swear they didn't give it to him."

"Maybe he got the point and he's done."

Lana reaches across the table, takes the dessert menu from my hands, and looks at me trying to figure out what I mean by that before she just straight-up asks.

"Would you be disappointed if he is?"

"I don't know. Maybe more disappointed that he backed down from you so easily."

"If he did, it's only because he got the message *I* don't want to see him. He doesn't know about you, Chanti. He isn't giving up on you. Besides, that might change once I do a little more digging."

"Suppose you don't find anything?"

"Yeah, right. You don't call me super cop for nothing. Well, except to be snarky."

"Speaking of," I say, glad Lana has given me an opening, "do you remember arresting a dude named Tragic last summer? It wouldn't have been long after you found MJ in that motel room on Colfax where her cousin was dealing."

I've been wanting to ask Lana this question ever since Donnell mentioned Tragic had been arrested by a cute lady cop. It likely would have been someone in Vice and there aren't many women in the Vice Squad. Lana is cute, so the odds are good.

"Tragic? Um . . . I don't . . . I'm not sure if that name rings a bell."

Lana picks up the dessert menu and starts looking it over, but unlike me, she probably won't be having dessert. She's not much on sweets, so I know she's using the menu as a cover, just like I had done a second ago. What I don't know is why Tragic's name makes her nervous.

"It isn't a typical name—seems like you'd remember a guy named Tragic."

"On the street, all the names are something like Tragic. Ask me about a guy named Bob or Richard and I could probably tell you every detail of the arrest. This brownie sundae looks good, don't you think?"

"Yeah, and I also think you remember all your arrests, even the ones with names like Tragic. Especially considering what he was trying to sell to undercover cops got him a tune-up."

"I wasn't involved in that tune-up. Internal Affairs cleared me," Lana says, giving up on trying to hide the fact she remembers Tragic's arrest. Or that it was so shady an IA investigation was opened on it. "How do you know about that case?"

I tell her what I learned about the deal going bad from Donnell without actually telling her that's where I got my information or that I'd visited him in prison today. When she assumes MJ somehow knew this information and shared it with me, I don't correct her.

"Now that you mention it, I remember Tragic being really surprised to find those drugs and armor-piercing bullets in his case."

"What had he expected to find?"

"I never found out. When the meet was arranged, there was never a discussion of any transaction taking place. We'd already met two of his soldiers—they set up the introduction."

That must have been Donnell and Lux.

"Tragic was the boss," Lana continues, "and we were just going to have a meet-and-greet, but he said he was excited to show us something. We were excited too—more like worried what he was about to bring out of that case, but we let him. There were three of us and one of him so it was safe. He acted as surprised as we were when he opened it."

"And he didn't tell you later, after you arrested him?"

"No, because like I said—his being surprised was an act. Cons lie, so he just kept saying he'd been double-crossed, but of course he wouldn't tell us by whom. He did promise several times to make retribution on whoever it was. Kind of hard to do from a prison cell, though."

"You'd think so, wouldn't you?" I say.

Chapter 25

I'm grateful for the full pot of coffee Lana left for me this morning and when I check the fridge for cream, I'm surprised by the turkey taking up a whole shelf. Oh yeah, that's right—it's the day before Thanksgiving. With everything going on, I completely forgot that's the reason I'm out of school this week. It's also just two days before my birthday and I have no party planned, no gift wish list made for Lana. With everything going on, it doesn't seem as important as it did a month ago.

I take my coffee in the living room and find the DVDs are still on the table where Marco left them. I didn't come up with any new ideas on MJ's case last night, but I do have a theory about these DVDs. At first I thought they were from Lux, though I hadn't thought up a reason why he'd send them to me. Then I thought it was a cute prank by Marco, but he swears he didn't send the package. I'm inclined to believe him because he isn't one to lie, even about a harmless prank. And if he really had sent the movies, it would have been so cute a prank that it bordered on being BF/GF-like, and we both agreed we wouldn't be going there.

So now I'm back to thinking it was Lux. But when I

looked through the box in MJ's basement, all the movies I saw were no older than a year or two. I suppose there could have been some ancient movies at the bottom of the box that I missed, but I can't imagine there's a huge market for movies that are older than my grandparents. And I still have no motive for Lux to send them, unless he just wants to taunt MJ after successfully setting her up to get arrested. But why send them to me?

When the doorbell rings and startles me out of my thoughts, I'm expecting it to be MJ since I told her I had some news to share after my little field trip yesterday, but by the time I open the door, there's no one there, just another envelope. It's padded like yesterday's package, but I can still feel the corners of DVD cases through the bubble wrap. I step out on the porch looking for signs of Lux. He isn't anywhere to be found, but I do see two squad cars roll up in front of MJ's house. Just as they get out of their cars, Lana pulls into our driveway and hurries up the porch.

"Come on, get inside," she says, rushing me into the house.

"What's going on?"

"I need to call Randolph Chatman."

"Why?"

"After what you told me at dinner last night, I got curious."

"Mom, that was just supposed to be us talking—I didn't think you were going to *do* anything."

"When you're talking to your mother, you're also talking to a cop. Your source suggested we may not have gotten the right man, or at least we didn't get him on the right charge. Since I'm too close to this case, I told Falcone to check it out. He and another detective went to Lux's place to ask him some questions."

"Don't tell me he skipped out."

"He's gone, but not of his own accord. His door was

busted in, his apartment ransacked. It looked like it may have just happened this morning."

"How could they tell?"

"Falcone found some blood in the apartment—fresh. There was also a neighbor who said she witnessed an altercation between Lux and a woman just two days ago. By her account, the woman fits MJ's description."

"So MJ was there and got into it with Lux. What does two days ago have to do with today?"

"The witness says the woman beat Lux up and threatened to kill him."

"Oh, please—she's exaggerating."

"How would you know?"

"I mean, who'd believe a woman beating up a guy?"

"Lux wasn't that big, and we both know MJ is capable. Not to mention the witness has photos of MJ about to choke Lux outside his apartment door."

Uh-oh. I guess now I know where that chick disappeared to so quickly while I was moving MJ's car out of her parking space. There's always somebody ready with a camera phone, just waiting for a chance to get on TV.

"Did you see the photos? I mean, was there anyone else in them besides MJ and Lux?"

"No, I don't think so. Why is that important?"

"Oh, just wondering if there were other witnesses, in case this one isn't reliable."

"You know, there might be. The witness said before MJ got into it with Lux, the witness was threatened by MJ after approaching her about parking in her assigned space. She says she feared for her life until another woman separated them and MJ left that fight to find Lux. Maybe we can find that other woman."

"You won't have to look very far," I say, realizing this isn't the time to try to keep Lana in the dark about how involved I am in this whole thing. "It was me."

"Oh no, Chanti," Lana says, shaking her head. "You're MJ's friend, you were there when she threatened him. You could be implicated."

"Implicated?"

"I need to call Randolph right now."

"Because the cops think MJ knows something about Lux's disappearance?"

"No. Because MJ is being taken in for questioning on the disappearance and suspected murder of Lux Trenton."

Chapter 26

By the time I'm showered and dressed, Lana has more bad news. After they took MJ away, they searched her house. They didn't find anything there, but there were bloody clothes in the trunk of Big Mama's car.

"How do they know the clothes have anything to do with Lux?" I say, even though I can't think of any good explanation for bloody clothes in MJ's trunk.

"All we know for sure is that they were men's clothes, but they're on the way to Forensics right now. There was one item that was pretty distinguishable—the gang unit is checking to see if it's a marking—"

"Don't tell me . . . brown hoodie, white scrollwork on the back?"

"That's it exactly. How in the world—"

"It's Lux's jacket. The first time I ever saw him he was wearing it."

"Chanti, what else haven't you told me?" Lana asks, using her cop interrogation voice that makes me feel like I could be joining MJ at the station.

"You said I could be implicated, but how? Because I was with MJ when she threatened Lux?"

"Depends on the witness's statement, how involved she

perceived you to be in the threat against Lux. As soon as the witness identifies you, you'll be part of the investigation. But we'll cross that bridge when we get to it. If we get to it. Now, your turn to give the answers. What else do you know?"

"Remember when I wanted to see the report on MJ's house fire? He was the guy I thought might have caused it. I've seen him hanging around the neighborhood a couple of times since."

"Well, that alone establishes a connection," Lana says.

I wonder how long before she figures out what the DH stands for on the back of that hoodie. Then she'll really see a connection and probably won't let me talk to MJ. Shoot— she may even put me in the box next door to MJ's interrogation room.

"Not enough connection to jump from Lux hanging around our street to MJ killing him."

"You putting him at the scene of her house fire gives her motive. I might not come to that conclusion if anyone but you were the witness who made him as the possible arsonist. Did you ever tell MJ your theory?"

Yeah, like fifty times, but I don't tell Lana that, not yet anyway, because I know MJ didn't kill Lux, even if she threatened to.

"Well, it doesn't look good for MJ. I'm pretty sure she won't be coming home tonight. The questioning is going to turn into an arrest as soon as the lab confirms the blood belongs to Lux."

"How much blood did they find in his apartment?"

"Too much for it to have been an accident, not enough for him to be dead—at least not when he left the apartment."

"MJ didn't do this, Mom."

"I know. At least, I want to believe that."

"After all she's done for me, even for you and the cops, you *have* to believe it."

"I know, honey, but MJ is a felon."

"*Ex*-felon, but I know how cops think. Once a bad guy, always a bad guy."

"The evidence looks—"

"Screw the evidence," I say, not even caring that I just said that to my mother. "I need to see MJ. Can you get me in?"

MJ looks as nervous as I've ever seen her, and police departments have never agreed with her. Even before this week, she's been here enough times to know the routine. This time her visit includes a possible murder charge.

"I can't believe I'm here again, Chanti. I swear, if I get out of this I will never talk to another con again, I don't care what dirt they have on me."

"*When* you get out, not if," I say. "Look, I told Lana I was there when that so-called witness saw you arguing with Lux. I'll make sure the cops know that chick was exaggerating, trying for her fifteen minutes of fame or getting back at you for always parking in her space. How often did you visit Lux, anyway?"

"I know that girl was pissed," MJ says without answering my question, "but who tries to send somebody up for charges this serious just because I parked in her space?"

"That wasn't all you did, MJ. You threatened her, too. Before I go to Lana, is there anything else I should know?"

By now, I know MJ well enough to know there is always something else—whether of her own doing or because of circumstance, that will undermine my investigation.

"It's pretty bad, Chanti. I don't have an alibi for the time they say I hurt Lux."

"You were home when they arrested you. They said it looked like Lux hadn't been gone long from his apartment when they got there."

"Yeah, but that was two hours before they actually came

to get me. You know how cops work. They had to check out the witness, talk to my probie, all that. So I had plenty of time to get home."

"You mean they could *say* you had plenty of time to get home. If Big Mama was home, she can vouch—"

"That's just it. I ain't got no alibi because I wasn't home. The same time they claim I was jacking up Lux, I was in the middle of nowhere waiting for him."

"Waiting for him?"

"Early this morning, I get a call from Lux saying to meet him outside this town called Limon."

"That's about an hour and a half southeast of here. There's nothing outside that town. There's barely anything inside."

"Yeah, that's what I found out. I waited nearly an hour for him on some dirt road that looked like it ain't seen a car in years, then came back to Denver. I wasn't home ten minutes when Five-O knocked on the door talking about they need to question me."

"What made you go all the way out there? You should have known Lux was up to something."

"Lux said he was going to set me free of all this, that he had some proof he could give me to clear my name with Tragic. But he was on his way out of Colorado, heading east."

"He couldn't give it to you here, before he left?"

"He was worried too many eyes might be on us in Denver. Plus he said he felt kind of bad about me getting arrested for the drug charge, said he wanted to clear that up before he dropped off the map."

"Right, Lux suddenly got a conscience after setting you up. You sure it was him on the phone?"

"Yeah, I know his voice. For the last few weeks, he's been calling me 24-7 threatening me about staying away from his box, so I definitely know his voice. It did sound a little different this morning though, but it was him."

"Different how?"

"I don't know, like he was nervous maybe."

"Probably because he was lying to you," I suggest. "At least we know he was alive this morning. He's probably still alive right now, even if that blood comes up as his. I heard it wasn't enough blood for him to be dead."

"You think this is just more of his trickeration?"

"This could be his way of putting everything on you, including his disappearance. Probably the only truthful thing he said was the part about getting out of town. Neither the cops nor Tragic will come looking for a dead Lux, especially if you're charged with killing him."

"A murder charge? Aw, damn, Chanti."

"It's gonna be okay. We're getting you out of this thing. Did you tell your lawyer what you told me?"

"He ain't come yet, but I will unless you think I shouldn't."

"No, tell him everything. Be completely straight. You've told me everything this time, right?"

"There's one more thing," MJ says, clenching her fists open and closed on the table between us.

"What?" I say, my stomach already starting to twist in knots.

"Remember how you was blowing up my voicemail the day Lux came for his box?"

"Yeah."

"What had happened was I had went over to his place to try to talk some sense into him."

"*Talk* some sense into him, MJ?"

"Talk . . . whatever. But he wasn't there, I guess because he was busy breaking into my house. Anyway, I didn't answer my phone because I was out looking for some protection from Lux. I knew if I talked to you I'd end up telling you what I was up to and you'd talk me out of it."

"What do you mean protection—like a gun?"

"Naw, I'm not stupid. That would violate my parole. But I know I guy who knows a guy. . . ."

"Oh, so you thought hiring someone to put a hurt on Lux was smarter than buying a gun? They're both felonies, MJ. I don't care if you hire someone to do it or if you do it yourself."

"I swear that's exactly what I heard you say in my head when I finally read all your texts and listened to your voice messages. I said to myself, 'Chanti would say this was a real bad idea.' That's what I said."

"And you were right."

"So I backed out of it, told the dude who knows the dude I know to leave it alone. I'm pretty sure he didn't do anything."

"Why are you so sure?"

"I never gave an order and I never paid him. Them kind of dudes never do anything for free."

"Unless he had beef with Lux, too. They weren't connected in any way, were they?"

"Not that I know of. Either way, I never told dude to kill Lux, just to scare him away."

"You could have done that yourself. That's what the witness and I pretty much saw you do."

"Okay, so I wanted to scare him with a little pain, make him think I had people. But just a little."

"You do have people—me and Lana and Big Mama. You should have come to us instead of looking for protection."

"I know, I know," MJ says, looking completely hopeless and not like she needs any more piling on from me. "Do I tell the lawyer this part, too?"

"Tell him *everything*. He can't help you unless he knows the whole story."

"Yeah, like that public defender helped me into a two-year juvie stint."

"Not all PDs are weak, and besides, Mr. Chatman isn't a PD. He's big-time lawyer Lana used to work for. Now he's her friend. He'll help you."

Like I conjured him up, Mr. Chatman arrives and that's my cue to leave. Before I go, I make sure he hears me tell MJ to tell him everything or I will, just so he doesn't worry she might be holding out on him because she's been talking to me. On my way out of the interrogation room, I run smack into a woman walking down the hall toward the exit. When I back up and apologize for almost mowing her down, I realize I know her. It's the witness whose testimony the police will probably use to charge MJ with murder. Instead of pointing me out to the nearest cop as the "woman" who broke up the fight between her and MJ over the parking space, she gives me the most sinister and knowing smile I've ever seen.

Now I get it. A real witness, one who clearly recognizes me, would have turned around and pointed me out. But she's headed for the door. She's working with Lux to set up MJ and I'm probably next. They'll tell the police I was with MJ that day making threats right along with her even though I tried to stop her. For whatever reason, they're playing a game of cat-and-mouse, dangling me by the tail like they're Tom and I'm Jerry. I have to move fast before they make their next play. Otherwise, Lana is right about me being implicated—as an accessory to murder, even if it's a staged murder that never really happened. Instead of looking forward to my birthday this weekend, I could be looking forward to sweet sixteen to life.

Chapter 27

I get home from the visit with MJ to find another mystery package leaning against my front door, this time a box instead of an envelope, but the labeling looks the same. Lux would have to be the boldest man on the planet to still be dropping these packages off "from the grave," so I call Marco to make absolutely sure he isn't behind this.

"I don't know who's sending the movies," Marco says when I question him, "but it isn't me. I told you Hitchcock is the director that made me think about going to film school. I'd never rip him off like that."

"Rip him off? What do you mean?"

"The DVDs I saw at your house the other day are bootlegs. I only knew they were Hitchcock films from the titles and the cover art. The art isn't original, either. Looks like someone just pulled stuff off the Net to make the covers."

Lux may be in hiding somewhere, playing dead, but that just means he's got someone else doing his dirty work. And he isn't just using me to taunt MJ.

"Marco, are you busy right now? And I mean right now."

"No, but—"

"Then I could really use your help. Can you come over?"

"What's going on?"

"MJ's case. This morning I thought it couldn't get much worse, but I was wrong. I think I might be the bad guy's next target."

While I'm on the phone with Marco, I realize the DVDs are part of whatever twisted game Lux is playing with me. When Marco gets to my house seven minutes later (I timed it and I have to say it's impressive—it's good to know I can count on him when my life is about to be totally screwed), I skip the small talk and tell him about the case as I make a pitcher of iced tea.

"That's why I need your help," I tell him after I've given him the quick version of everything, going back to the fire at MJ's house. "I think Lux is a film buff and he's using these DVDs to send me some kind of clue of how he's setting me up. I really hope you won't give me a hard time about the whole playing-detective thing."

"Of course I'll help you. But I won't lie, Chanti—I think it's dangerous what you're doing and I think you need to call the police—"

"But I *know* the police. . . I mean . . ."

Lana's secret is one I need permission to tell, so I tell him the part that I can.

"My mom, she's a paralegal and she knows a lot about the law and crime and stuff. And the attorney she works for has agreed to be MJ's lawyer, so the police are involved. I'm just trying to help MJ and—"

"Chanti, if you'd let me finish, it's dangerous and better left for the police, but I won't let you get hurt, either." Our hands touch when he takes the glass of iced tea from me, just like the time with the mug of cocoa.

"Yeah?" is all I manage to say.

"Yeah. I'll be your backup. No matter what."

I know it's crazy that I have a bad guy trying to railroad

me and my friend is about to be charged with murder, but right now I want nothing more than to throw my arms around Marco and let him hold me until all the crazy disappears. I wish it were that easy. I wish he didn't have a girlfriend, or that I wasn't a menace to his family. From the way he's looking at me, I'm beginning to wonder if he's thinking the same thing. Then he steps away from me suddenly, taking his drink into the living room, where we left the DVDs.

"What I don't get is why play this game?" Marco says as he looks through the DVDs. "I mean, if he's faked his disappearance or death, and it's looking bad for MJ, why do this? Why help you out by sending clues? You'd think he'd be spending energy on making sure the case against MJ sticks."

"Maybe that's what these DVDs are for—the nail in the coffin for MJ. Or for me. What if they aren't clues and he just wants me to have them when the cops come knocking and find my fingerprints all over them the same way he set up MJ when he switched these movies out for drugs?"

"No, I think you were right about them being clues to something. If he was trying to plant evidence from the grave or wherever he's hiding out, he'd have sent them all at once. He's sending some kind of message by doling them out like this."

I smile at him, completely impressed. "You're kind of good at this, you know."

"Well, I can't let you go to jail. Who else would I hang out with at Langdon?"

"Unlike me, you've made a lot of friends at school. I'm the social outcast, remember?"

"Those are just people I know, they aren't friends. Besides, I think you know you're more than that to me, even if we did agree—"

"Okay, so maybe we should start watching these," I say, jumping off the sofa to put a DVD in the player. I don't want to hear what he has to say or deal with another awkward moment of looking longingly into his eyes knowing I can't have him or what to do with him if I could.

"Hold up before you put the movie in. I was so worried about checking on you, I completely forgot I have food in the car. I was on my way home from picking up a pizza when you called."

Is it weird that with everything going on, I'm kind of tingling like this is a date? Even worse, I'm glad it's happening. Not the Lux and MJ part, but the part where Marco and I are about to share a pizza on the same sofa to watch movies for clues. Yep, I'm officially crazy.

"We gotta eat," Marco says, apparently reading my mind.

"That's true. I'll walk out with you. The cold air might clear my head a little and help me think."

When we get out on the street, I don't see his car.

"Where'd you park?"

"In front of a house a few doors down. I couldn't find a space any closer."

"That reminds me of something I've wanted to ask since the last time you dropped by. I've never given you my address and you hadn't been here before, so how'd you know where I lived?"

"Okay, so I creeped on you a little. I looked you up in the student directory the first week we were at Langdon."

"Oh yeah?" I say, trying to sound nonchalant when really I remember coming home the day I met Marco and spending three hours online finding everything I could on him. The student directory is the one thing I didn't check.

"I hope I get points for telling you that. It isn't something a guy likes to admit."

"You get points, but I don't know what you'll use them on. It isn't like we're together, or anything."

"I'm here. You're here. If you look it up, that's probably the definition of together."

The way he's looking at me makes me think he might be breaking the rules of our platonic agreement and there's more going on between us than solving a case. It also makes me feel like a boyfriend thief, so I break our gaze

We're walking back from his car, the pizza still warm enough to create a little cloud of steam around the box, when we see a kid on a bike pull up in front of my house, throw his bike down, and run up to my porch. Under his arm is a familiar-looking package.

Chapter 28

By the time we reach the house, the kid is moving fast and already back down the stairs and about to mount his bike.

"He must be Lux's courier," I say quickly.

Marco hands me the pizza box and grabs the kid before he can ride off. Good thing because Marco needs both hands free to block the small fists being wildly thrown his way. He packs a punch for a kid I guess to be about eight or nine.

"Hey, little man, I'm not going to hurt you. We just want to know who gave you that box to drop off."

The boy stops hitting and squirming long enough to point at me.

"I know you. Sometimes I see you waiting at the bus stop on Center Street when I'm riding my bike. You live here?"

"I do. And that's my name on the package. So you want to tell me who my secret admirer is?"

This seems to relax the kid enough to trust we don't plan to do him any harm, though Marco still doesn't let go of the boy's bike.

"A man up the street."

"He lives up the street?" I ask.

"No. He was parked on the corner a minute ago, near the dry cleaner's. He gave me ten dollars to deliver this package and the other ones, too. My mom works at the dry cleaner's, so I hang around there. I told him my mother only lets me ride my bike on the sidewalk, and I have to stay on the block."

I pull my phone from my pocket and search for the photo I took of Lux the day I caught him taking the box out of MJ's house.

"Was this the guy?"

"Nah, nothing like that. He was bigger and taller. More like his size," he says, pointing to Marco. "Wait, one time he was with another guy, and I think that might be him."

"Do you remember what the car looked like?" I ask.

"Uh, I just saw it a minute ago," the kid says like I must think he's stupid. "It's nothing special, 'cept it had a rental car sticker on the bumper. I noticed 'cause the sticker was neon green, like my bike."

"But the smaller guy wasn't with him today?" Marco asks.

"Nope. Big dude was with a lady this time. She was real pretty, with a funny tattoo under one eye, like she was crying."

I thank the boy and Marco gives him his bike back, along with ten dollars not to mention our conversation if he ever sees the man again.

"What do you think?" Marco asks as we watch the boy pedal away.

"I only ever saw Lux drive a car once—when he switched out the DVDs with drugs and got MJ busted the first time. It also had a neon-green rental car sticker on it. I have no idea who the mystery man is driving the car today, but I know who the pretty lady with the funny tattoo is."

"Yeah? Who?"

"The alleged witness to the altercation between Lux and MJ. The kid just confirmed for me that she's working with Lux."

"You kill me how you talk like you know this stuff. Then again, history proves you actually do know this stuff."

"I told you, I watch a lot of cop shows. And now I guess I'll be watching a lot of old movies."

On the way into the house, I pick up the latest DVD shipment the kid left at the door.

"Where do we start?" Marco asks.

"I think you were right about him having a reason to dole them out to us like it's part of the game, so he probably wants us to watch them in the order we received them."

"That's a problem because I think I mixed them up when I was looking through them."

"That's okay. I have a great memory," I say, taking the packages into the dining room. "I'll just group them on this table based on which package they came in, the order they were stacked inside the package, and the time I received each group."

"You even remember the order they were stacked inside the box? I hope you know you can never use the excuse with me that you forgot we had a date . . . or you forgot to call me, or something like that."

I pretend I didn't hear the slip and focus on getting the wrapper off the first DVD. When I finally get it open, I'm surprised to find the case empty.

"Why'd he send us an empty case?" I ask, not expecting Marco to actually know the answer. "Now we'll start off with a missing clue. I hope these clues aren't like math and you have to build on the one before it."

"That's okay. I've seen *The Wrong Man* a couple of times," Marco says. "Open the next one."

I do and it's empty, too. So are the rest of the cases, all of them sealed up tight and nearly impossible to get into, only to find there's nothing inside.

"I'm starting to hate Lux and I definitely hate being played with."

"Wait a minute," Marco says, looking a lot less confused than I am. "I get it. It's the titles he's giving us, not the movies themselves. The titles are the clues. That's why he sent them in a certain order, and why he sent them empty. You probably don't even need a Hitchcock movie buff to figure this out."

"Uh-uh, you aren't going anywhere. You've already figured out more than I ever would have."

Marco not only doesn't go anywhere, he stands so close to me as I line up the DVDs again that I'm having a hard time remembering the order. Now I know what can make my great memory go haywire—Marco's touch.

"I told you I have your back. I'm not leaving, just pointing out how the clues might be easier and faster to solve than we thought."

His proximity is making it hard for me to think, so I step a few feet away from him.

"So they're lined up again based on the order they came. Let's look for a pattern," I say, hoping I sound about as unfeeling and clinical as if I were giving a presentation in my AP chemistry class, when really I'm totally flustered.

Group One	Group Two	Group Three
The Wrong Man	I Confess	To Catch a Thief
Suspicion	Saboteur	North By Northwest
Sabotage	Blackmail	The Birds
		Number 17
		Topaz
		Rear Window
		Torn Curtain

"So you're telling me you've never seen any of these movies," Marco asks as though I've never seen a full moon.

"No, but a few in the last column sound familiar. Once MJ and I are off the hook for murder, I promise we . . . I will watch every one of them, okay?" Oops. I keep talking as a cover. "Isn't this the same guy who did *Psycho?*"

"There's hope for you yet."

"That's probably the most famous one of all. Why not include it?"

"Because it doesn't make sense as a clue for whatever it is we're supposed to figure out. Or maybe it's true what they say about crazy people. They're the last to know. Maybe he didn't use it because he doesn't realize he's psycho."

As I listen to Marco and look over the groups, I realize he's on to something even though he was joking.

"He may not think he's psycho," I say, "but what if he thinks he's *The Wrong Man?*"

"And he *suspects sabotage?*"

"Then it wouldn't be Lux using the tall man and the pretty lady to deliver the DVDs from the grave. The only people who have been sabotaged in this whole thing are MJ and Donnell—by Lux—but they're both in jail."

"What if the tall man and the pretty lady are delivering these on their own, not on Lux's behalf? Maybe they've been sabotaged too," Marco suggests.

"Possibly. The tall man's identity is a mystery, but I think the pretty lady is working for Lux, pretending to be a neighbor who conveniently witnessed MJ threatening him. For now, I'm sticking with the assumption Lux is behind this."

"If I can believe what I see in movies, if people in jail can put hits on their enemies, I'm guessing they can get boxes of DVDs delivered to people."

"That's true, but usually they need to have been well-connected before they went in, something MJ and Donnell aren't," I explain, not even caring if Marco asks how I can be such an authority on convicts. Luckily he's so into reading the clues, he doesn't.

"Seems like Lux falls more in the second group of DVDs—he's the *Saboteur* who put both MJ and Donnell in jail, and he ran a *Blackmail* game on MJ to stash the DVDs. But I doubt we'll be hearing Lux say *I Confess* anytime soon."

"Especially if we can't find him," I say. "Maybe that one's in there as a trick question or a taunt. What about the third group? Not a single suggestion of a crime or wrongdoing like we had in the first two sets."

"The first one is, *To Catch a Thief.*"

"But there was no theft in all of this. We had blackmail and sabotage, but no theft."

"Uh, whoever created these bootlegs is a thief. That's Lux, right?"

"Marco, that's brilliant," I say, remembering something Lana had said this morning: *We may not have gotten the right man.*

"Can you tell me why I'm so brilliant?"

"There is one other player in this whole thing, and he has enough juice to be running this from inside—Tragic. He was the head of the Down Home gang until Lux set him up and sent him to jail. I thought Lux was running this, faking his death so he can get MJ arrested and get clear of any retribution from Tragic. But what if Tragic is the mastermind?"

"Okaay . . . if you say so. This is your world. I'm just along for the ride."

"Lux didn't create the bootlegs," I explain, "but he stole them from the person who did—Tragic. When Lux made the switch before Tragic's meet with my . . . I mean, with some undercover cops, I bet he exchanged the DVDs with cop-killer bullets. That way he could send Tragic to prison, take over the Down Homes, and go into the bootleg business himself."

"Seems like a good plan, I mean, as far as gang domination plans go."

"But it didn't go as planned for Lux. According to Donnell, Lux's vision was bigger than his capabilities, and he was run out of Los Angeles by his gang. Lux is originally from here, he knows the town, he knows MJ. He came to Denver looking to start up his own operation."

"Okay, I get it," Marco says. "That's why Lux needed to keep the DVDs hidden away in MJ's basement until he could make more copies and sell them. He was on probation and didn't want to be caught in possession of the DVDs. And if any Down Homes caught him with the DVDs, it would be revealed Tragic was set up by Lux, not MJ."

"Exactly," I say, impressed with how good Marco is at the sleuthing thing. "Then Lux realized Tragic had figured him out, ran out of time, and had to destroy the DVDs instead, because they were evidence. That means Lux is the thief, not the wrong man. And if Tragic is behind this, Lux may not be faking his death. He may really be in trouble."

"You're thinking the tall man and the pretty lady are working for Tragic?" Marco asks.

"Yep, and they're probably behind the blood the cops found in Lux's apartment. We never looked at the last envelope the kid just brought," I say.

"We should have asked the kid whether he knew if there were any more coming," Marco says.

When I open the envelope with the latest DVD, I see it's the most critical clue of all.

"I think this might be the last clue."

"Why? Which movie is it?"

I hold it up for him to see.

"*Murder!*"

Chapter 29

When I send Lana a 911 text that she needs to come home, she responds that she's in the area and just ten minutes away. By the time she arrives, Marco and I—well, pretty much just Marco— figured out the third set of movie titles are clues to Lux's location.

When Lana walks in to find Marco there, she doesn't look too happy.

"Hi, Marco. Um, Chanti, can I see you in the kitchen for a second?"

I follow her out of the dining room. "Mom, Marco and I—"

"Exactly. I'm glad you and your friend are . . . friends again, but you know I don't allow boys up in here when I'm not home."

"I know, but he's been helping me solve these clues from the DVDs. I think we've figured out where Lux might be. We don't think he's dead."

"Whoa, back up," Lana says, walking back into the dining room, where Marco is still looking over the third group of titles. "What's going on and how much does this one know?"

Marco looks up to see if he's the "this one" Lana is referring to.

"It's okay. Marco knows you're a paralegal and your boss is defending MJ."

"Oh—right, okay."

"I'm glad Chanti finally told me about you being a paralegal. It explains a lot about why she's kind of obsessed with crime-solving," Marco says.

"Yeah, but paralegals don't solve crimes. We leave that *to the police.*"

"That's what I keep telling her, Ms. Evans."

"So she doesn't listen to you, either? Maybe if we both keep trying . . ."

I'm glad to see Lana and Marco are having a bonding moment over my recalcitrance, but we really need to find Lux before it's too late for him, MJ, and possibly me. I bring Lana up to speed on everything, right up to where Marco has figured out Tragic is holding Lux somewhere near the Denver Zoo.

"How did you get the Denver Zoo out of this?" Lana asks, waving her hand over the table full of DVDs.

"First he tells us this third set of DVDs are instructions *To Catch a Thief.* His general location is *North by Northwest.*"

"That could be the whole northwestern corner of the city, state, or country for that matter."

"No, Lux is close by," I say. "My theory is this is a game with Tragic. He wants to see if he can be caught so he's going to make sure the possibility exists. And for some reason, it's me he wants to play the game with. We think Tragic is saying Lux is northwest of *me.*"

I think I might know the reason Tragic wants to play this game with me—he knows I busted Donnell, Lux probably told him I was on to him as early as the fire, and now he wants to see if I can catch him. Fortunately Lana is too deep into deciphering the clues to ask why I think Tragic sent these clues to me, or maybe she's figured it out for herself.

"Okay, what does this next clue mean?" Lana asks.

"*The Birds?*" Marco asks. "We got online and figured out we don't have an aviary in the area, but we remembered the zoo has Bird World. All those grade-school field trips—never thought they'd help me find a killer."

"Let's hope he isn't a killer yet," I say. "At least not of Lux."

"I'm starting to see it now," Lana says, looking at the third group of DVDs. "The zoo is northwest of where we are, and the zoo is inside City Park, which is bordered by Seventeenth Avenue. *Number 17.* That's in my zone."

"Yes, where your law office is," I say, surprised Lana made that slip in front of Marco. But I can tell she's really getting into the clues.

"Wow, this is good work, Marco," she says.

Uh, hello? I helped.

"So what did you get for *Topaz?*"

"I was just getting to that one," I say. "It stumped me for a second because I was looking for Topaz on the map—a street, a restaurant name, a housing subdivision. But I'd heard Tragic had a meth operation, and figured he might know his chemistry."

"If I remember right, that's how he got started in his life of crime, as a meth cook." Lana stops and looks at Marco. "I read that in the paper, a story about his arrest a while back. Some of those guys do know science. What about this clue made you think of that?"

"The chemical composition of topaz gives it a crystalline structure," I explain. "It's one of the less stable silicates— which is kind of funny since Tragic doesn't seem too stable either, right?" Marco and Lana are looking at me like they don't get the joke. "Anyway, topaz is a crystal, and on Seventeenth Avenue, right across from City Park, are the Crystal Pointe Apartments."

"Take a look," Marco says, passing my laptop to Lana. "In *Rear Window,* Jimmy Stewart thinks he witnessed a murder take place from the rear window of his apartment. This clue doesn't match exactly because you can't see City Park from a rear window of any Crystal Pointe Apartment."

"We checked it on Google Earth," I explain. "If there weren't a bunch of trees in the way, an apartment facing Seventeenth Avenue would have a perfect view of Bird World. We think that's the part Tragic is trying to tell us."

"And *Torn Curtain*?"

"Look for an apartment window with a torn curtain? That's all we could come up with for that one," Marco says.

"But the most important DVD is this last one. *Murder!* I think Tragic has added a ticking clock to this game," I explain. "We need to find Lux before he's killed. Marco and I just did a pretty sweet job of figuring out these clues, but it's still all a hunch. It'll sound completely crazy in court if MJ is charged for murder."

"But how can MJ be charged if she's been in jail all day?" Marco asks.

"It depends on how Tragic plans to kill Lux," Lana says. "To be able to blame it on MJ, Lux was probably hurt this morning about the time she was in Limon waiting for him to show up, when Tragic took away any alibi she may have had."

I add, "Prosecution will say she hurt him before her arrest and left him for dead, when really Lux might be in an apartment across from City Park, being finished off by the pretty lady and the tall man."

Despite Marco's protest, we leave him at the house in case more DVDs arrive to be deciphered. For someone who wants nothing to do with detective stuff, he sure seems like he wants to get involved. But Lana tells him his parents probably wouldn't appreciate it, and all Lana is going to do is relay the information to MJ's lawyer. When Marco asks why we can't just call the lawyer, neither Lana nor I try to come up with a story for that. We just leave and tell him to call us if any more packages arrive or if he thinks of any new clues.

The minute we get in the car, Lana radios to Falcone to meet her at the Crystal Pointe Apartments, along with a couple of black-and-whites.

"I should have left you back there with Marco," Lana says.

"I thought you didn't want me at the house alone with a boy."

"Don't get smart."

"Admit it, Lana—you need me. I might figure out more clues on the way. We can find Lux a whole lot faster if I can direct you to his precise location instead of knocking on every apartment door."

She doesn't respond, which means I'm right. We drive in silence for a few minutes.

"Mom, I know it's a weird time to bring this up with everything that's going on, or maybe it's a good time with all that's going on, but I can't help but think about him . . . my father. Did you find anything on him yet?"

"Yes."

"What?"

"Nothing. I found out nothing at all."

"Why'd you say yes, then?"

"Because nothing is *something*. I have access to all kinds of records—NCIC, prison, birth, death—and I couldn't find a damn thing."

"What does that mean?"

"I don't know. It's like he doesn't exist. Few people on the planet get to disappear, and they tend to work with some very secret offices based in Washington. Maybe he's black ops for the government," Lana says, adding a laugh. That means my father's disappearance—on paper, at least—has spooked her. Lana always laughs off the few things that ever frighten her.

Since things that scare Lana have a tendency to completely freak me out, I return to thinking about the movie titles, something I can handle. Before we left the house, I took a picture of the table with the DVDs with my phone. I have an eidetic memory—what most people call photographic—but I didn't want to rely on just that for something this important. I can't find any more clues in the titles, so I zoom out to look at the whole table and the rows of DVDs. Marco was right about the order Tragic sent the DVDs being a clue, and I think there are clues in the order to more than just Tragic's reason for running this whole game or Lux's location.

When we arrive at the Crystal Pointe Apartments, I see that I'm probably right. The building has three stories.

"Lana, he's on the third floor. If there's an apartment number 337, that's where he'll be."

"Where'd you get that?"

"The DVDs—he sent them in four groups, three in the first two packages, seven in the next, and one in the final delivery."

"What about the last number—the *one?*"

"This place is too small for a four-digit apartment number, but it's just a guess."

"No, this is good. We can start with that, looking for apartment 337," Lana says as Falcone pulls in, followed by two uniforms. "Stay here. I wish I hadn't let you talk me into bringing you."

"Bringing me helped, didn't it? I'll be okay. If Lux is really in there dying, the tall man and pretty lady—or whoever did this job for Tragic—are long gone. They don't want to be caught, just like Tragic wouldn't be playing this game if he weren't already serving a life term. He has nothing to lose. Whoever is working for him does."

"Just the same, stay put until I get back."

As soon as I promise to stay put and Lana is gone behind the building, the half a pitcher of iced tea I had at the house while Marco and I were clue-solving becomes a problem. Now I know why Lana always says a Big Gulp before a stake-out is a very bad idea. I guess all the adrenaline pumping through me as Lana drove across town like a bat out of hell kept me from noticing before, but now I *really* have to go. I spot a gas station two blocks down the street and get out of the car. But I never make it there.

Chapter 30

I'm halfway to the gas station—a block between there and the apartment complex—when a car pulls up to the curb a few yards ahead of me. Before I can register the neon-green rental car sticker on the bumper, someone in a full Halloween mask opens the door, grabs me, and pulls me into the backseat before the driver takes off. The woman at the wheel turns to look at me, and I see it's the pretty lady. I could swear her teardrop tattoo was under her right eye, but it must be under her left eye, on the side of her face I can't see. I suppose even *my* memory could fail me at a time like this.

I assume it's Lux sitting next to me, that I've gotten all the Hitchcock clues wrong and he's alive and well, but I don't want to find out. It's bad enough I already know who the driver is. Bad guys tend to kill you once you know their identity. But dude pulls the mask off and I see that I was definitely wrong about one thing.

"Cisco?"

"Don't be afraid."

"Where are we going?"

"Someone wants to talk to you."

"Who?"

"I think you already know."

"Lux? So he's alive?"

Cisco ignores my question. I pay attention to our route in case I get a chance to call for help, but in the meantime, I try my best to act like I'm not worried. Maybe Cisco really does want to just talk. No need for me to make him nervous or set him off by freaking out. Not that I have much time for freaking out—at least not in the car. We only go a couple of miles before we pull into the driveway of a house.

Lana always told me to never get into a bad guy's car. Once you're in the car, it's over. Better to make them kill you on the street than wherever it is they plan to take you. I wasn't given a choice whether to get into this car, but I can fight going into that house. I'm sure the car rule applies to letting bad guys take you into strange houses, but somehow, I don't think Cisco will hurt me.

That time we spoke at the bus stop, he actually acted like he owed me something, like we shared a secret. After he pulled me into the car, I never heard the click of the doors locking. My window was partially open on the short drive to this house. We drove city blocks and stopped at traffic lights. I could have tried to jump out or screamed for help at any time. And when we pulled into the driveway and the pretty lady put the car in park and turned around to get her instructions from Cisco, I wasn't wrong about which eye had the teardrop tattoo. There is no tattoo. It was a fake.

So when Cisco leads me out of the car and asks if I'm going to give him any trouble, I tell him no.

When we walk inside the small house, we're standing in a living room with a bar. There's a man at the bar with his back to us. He's fixing himself a drink; I hear the ice clink in a glass. Cisco, who has been holding one of my arms until now, grabs the other one and zip-ties my hands behind my back.

"Just a precaution," he says, and I immediately regret underestimating his level of bad-guy-ness.

"Really, Cisco? How afraid can you be of a sixteen-year-old girl?"

"Not yet," says the guy at the bar, still working on his drink.

"What?"

"You aren't sixteen *yet.*"

"How do you know—who are you?"

"I know your birthday isn't for another two days, and you know what they say about assumptions."

"Who is this guy, Cisco?" I ask, because he's too tall to be Lux.

That's when he turns around and I see he has a patch over his left eye. At first I think he's gone a little overboard with the bad-guy routine, but then I realize he isn't wearing the patch just to look menacing.

"Tragic?"

"Now, let's start again, shall we? Hello, Chanti. Nice to meet you."

"Shouldn't you be in prison?"

Tragic ignores my question. "I hope my man treated you well."

"Cisco's your man? But how—I mean, when—did he get involved?"

"Me and my girl been involved ever since Donnell brought me on board last summer to help him set up a Denver operation of the Down Homes. Well, that was the plan before you took him down," Cisco says, speaking for the first time since he cuffed my hands. "Like I said, I appreciated that."

"Not enough, apparently." I'm scared, but I can't help but be a smartass. It's how I calm myself enough to figure a way out of situations like this. Sadly, I've been here before.

"After Tragic was sent to prison, and Donnell went inside, Tragic knew Lux was returning to Denver and saw me as an opportunity to get to Lux for setting him up," Cisco explains.

"No one is going to believe MJ or I were behind Lux's murder. Is that why he sounded nervous this morning when he called MJ—because you had him and were forcing him to make that call to send MJ off to Limon, with no alibi?"

"Lux's murder?" Tragic asks.

"I get why you went after Lux, but why MJ?" I ask Tragic, trying to sound cooler than I really am. "Was she just collateral damage?"

Cisco answers instead. "By the time Tragic put his plan into place, Lux had already involved MJ, hiding the box in her house and setting her up with her probation officer. I wanted to stay out of it since Lux already knew who I was through Donnell. But I guess you knew me and Lux were acquaintances since you were spying on us that night at your girl Michelle's house."

"No way you saw me that night," I say, but obviously he did. I guess my creeping skills aren't as tight as I thought. "Did Lux notice me?"

"No, he isn't as observant as I am," Cisco says, doing that weird we-share-a-secret smile again. "So I could stay clear of Lux, I had Golden—my girl—start hustling him, pretending to be a neighbor with a romantic interest. But I got pulled into it anyway when MJ came to me looking for a hitter to rough up Lux."

"That was you she was meeting with?"

"Yeah. You were blowing her phone up that day. Good thing she didn't answer. You might have kept her from coming to me. Turns out it was a game I needed to be in on, after all."

"So, Tragic, you think MJ was part of the double-cross? Because you're wrong."

"Actually, both of you are wrong. MJ matters as much to me as Lux does—not at all."

"So why am I here?" I ask. "What's this about?"

"It's about you. You're the only one I wanted. The others were just a means to an end. Actually, so are you."

"What did I ever do to you? You don't even know me."

"But I do know your mother."

"What's going on here, man?" Cisco interrupts. "I thought we just gonna use her to get to MJ, to make MJ tell us what she knows about Lux and them bullets that put you away."

"I know all about both of you," Tragic continues. "You're a smart girl to get all those clues I sent."

"Why did you send them, anyway? To lead me to Lux—or to you?"

"Both—and just for kicks. The usual methods—a drive-by, paying someone to do a hit on all of you—wouldn't have been as much fun. I love Hitchcock, and I thought you'd get the connection between Lux, the DVDs, and how he set me up. You did not disappoint. I bet you'd make a better cop than your mother. Not that you'll ever get the chance."

Until now, I'd forgotten all about the reason I'd left Lana's car in the first place, but suddenly that half pitcher of iced tea is screaming again. Death threats will do that to you.

"Tragic, let's stay focused on getting the name of the arms dealer Lux got those cop-killers from," Cisco says. "If we get that, the feds are happy, your sentence is reduced, I keep the business going 'til you get out, everything's all good."

"Nothing is 'all good' until I get that cop who took out my eye," Tragic says.

"Think about it, Tragic. We're so close now. We got Lux hemmed up. Not only is MJ facing life, we'll be sending her best friend back with the message that this is serious. Eventually one of 'em is gonna talk. Just gotta stay focused."

Tragic is focused, but not on what Cisco's talking about. "So, should we make that call to your mother now?"

"Internal Affairs cleared her of that tune-up."

"Internal Affairs," Tragic says like you'd say the word *maggots*. Or *Brussels sprouts*. "The granddaddy of all snitches. I trust them about as much as I trust . . . well, I don't trust anyone."

A look passes between Cisco and Tragic, and if I wasn't completely terrified before, I am now.

"Let's go, Chanti," Cisco says, leading me to the door.

"She's not going anywhere. Neither are you, Cisco," Tragic says, reaching for something on the bar behind him, and I can only guess it's a gun. Cisco pushes me away and the front door crashes open. The first time I met the pretty lady, I cursed her for being so stealthy. Now I'm grateful because before Tragic can grab his gun and raise it, Golden gets off a shot.

Chapter 31

I didn't know if Tragic was hit or not, or how bad, and I don't even care. I'm just glad Cisco and I are hustling back into the rental car and Golden is sliding behind the wheel. My heart begins to slow to a normal pace as I realize we're heading back toward the Crystal Pointe Apartments.

"Is he dead?" I finally ask Cisco.

"Does it matter?"

I'm about to suggest that we should at least call the police. If he's dead or dying, I suppose it doesn't matter. If he's alive, that means he can still come after me and Lana. And it looks like Cisco's now on his hit list too. But I know better than to suggest that to bad guys, even ones who saved my life. I mean, after they almost got me killed in the first place.

"Thanks for not letting the crazy man kill me."

"Aurora Ave people have to look out for their own, right?"

"I wish you'd thought of that before you took me in there."

"I didn't know he wanted to kill you. I thought he just wanted to use you to send a message to MJ."

"MJ doesn't know anything about an arms supplier. If Lux got those cop-killers, he did it on his own."

"I know that now."

"But MJ's in jail. And Lux—"

"Lux is alive. The police will find him soon, and MJ will be exonerated."

"What about you? All of this so you can keep Lux off your territory?"

"At first that was the reason. If there was going to be a Down Homes operation in Denver, I wanted to be the one to run it. Then Tragic offered me an opportunity in Los Angeles. He needed someone to run his operation until he got out."

"I guess that's the least of Tragic's worries now," I say.

"Time will tell."

This is a lot like our conversation at the bus stop that day. Cisco gets a kick out of being mysterious.

"What you said back there about the feds reducing his sentence in return for information. Was Tragic out of prison because he's working as a confidential informant?"

"The man was right when he said you were smart. Maybe too smart for your own good."

"Well, all I have to say is Tragic has a really bad handler."

"Handler?"

"I watch TV. And my mom *is* a cop, as you apparently know. What kind of handler lets his CI get hold of a gun and just run off and do his own thing? I mean, seriously, dude needs some extra training or something."

Cisco just smiles at me, and I even get a tiny chuckle out of Golden, who except for being an excellent shot, has been quiet the whole time.

I stay quiet and start replaying everything that's happened in the last twenty-two minutes. Seems like a lot longer, but that's what the clock on the dashboard is telling me how long it's been since I got out of Lana's car. I think about Golden and her fake tattoo, the unlocked doors and open window. And how Cisco didn't zip-tie my hands until after we were inside that house. If I required such a "precaution," why not do it when he first put me in the car?

"You sound different," I say. "I mean, not like that time we talked at the bus shelter."

"You mean the ghetto-speak?"

"Yeah, and using words like *exonerated*."

"Not everything on the street is as it seems."

I don't speak cryptic, but when we pull in front of the Crystal Pointe Apartments, I decide I can live with not knowing all the details for once. I just want out of this car. When Golden stops at the curb, I don't ask permission; I just jump out. But instead of walking away, I lean into the still open window.

"Just one last question, Cisco. Are you true blue?"

He doesn't answer, just gives me that weird smile that now makes a lot of sense. Golden drives away.

Chapter 32

I was back in Lana's car just a minute or two before she re-
turned, and made her take me to that gas station, and no, I
couldn't wait until we got to headquarters. I still haven't told
Lana about Cisco, but I will tomorrow. I'll probably have to
make a statement at the police station, and even though I don't
believe Cisco is a threat because he's probably undercover himself, Lana needs to know her cover is blown. All that can wait
until tomorrow. I figure we've both had enough for tonight.

Cisco was right; Lux was alive, if not well. Falcone found
him in apartment 337 just like I said, in a chair with his hands
and feet tied to it. Someone had roughed him up pretty bad,
and he had a dead rat hanging around his neck, the box of
DVDs at his feet. There had been some additions to the box
since I'd looked inside—several boxes of cop-killer bullets
and a list of all Lux's unsolved arson cases, including MJ's
house. An anonymous call was made to the police directing
them to Tragic, who was in critical condition, last I heard.

We left Mr. Chatman and Big Mama at the police station,
but they'll be bringing MJ home any minute. Cisco was right
about that, too.

By the time Lana and I get home from the station, it's after
midnight. I'm hoping I find Marco still here, but he's gone.

"Did I tell you Big Mama invited us to have potluck dinner down at their place? Sort of a welcome home for MJ. I'm too wired to go to sleep. Might as well start cooking for tomorrow," Lana says, heading for the kitchen. "I mean today."

I follow her into the kitchen. I guess she isn't the only one too wired to sleep.

"Want some help?" I ask.

"Oh, you've already given me a ton of help, you and Marco. Good work tonight."

Lana stops pulling food out of the refrigerator to look at me.

"Are you and he—"

"Just friends."

"He's a good kid. I like him."

"Yeah, so do I."

"You never know. Sometimes these things work out."

"I thought you were worried about me having a boyfriend."

"All mothers worry about that."

"You more than most," I remind her.

"True, but I have to heed my own advice, what I told you at your friend Bethanie's going-away party. You and Marco aren't your father and me."

A party. A father. Two things it appears I won't be having anytime soon.

"Speaking of—still no word on that front?" I ask, already knowing the answer.

"Not yet."

"We shouldn't have changed the number. We haven't heard from him since."

"He found us the first time. He can do it again—if he wants to."

"Not if he knows you'll just turn him away."

"I won't next time," Lana says. She must see that this isn't the right answer, that it's not nearly enough, because she adds, "We won't wait for him to call us. I'll figure out what his true story is now and I'll find him. I promise you that, Chanti."

Chapter 33

Friday morning, I slept in with a too-much-turkey-and-dressing hangover. But that wasn't the only reason I stayed in bed late. The first thing I saw when I woke up was the dress still hanging on the back of my door with nowhere to go. More time asleep meant less time thinking about starting the lamest sixteenth birthday ever. It took me a few seconds to notice the sticky note attached to the clear plastic dress bag. The note was in Lana's handwriting.

Be on the front porch at noon. Wear me.

Now it's a couple of minutes before noon and I'm waiting on the porch, shivering, because I refuse to cover up my gorgeous dress with a coat. But I'm carrying a coat anyway because I know Lana will fuss if I don't. I've gotten used to the idea there won't be a party, but at least I'll get lunch. And there's no way this dress is going to the Cheesecake Factory, no matter how good the Godiva Chocolate Cheesecake is. This birthday, I'm picking someplace special. That's what I'm thinking when Marco pulls in front of my house on a motorcycle. No, not a motorcycle—one of those scooter things. What the . . . ?

"You ready?" Marco says. "Wow, you look . . . beautiful."

I'm so surprised to see him, I forget to thank him and say, "You're taking me to lunch? I thought my mom . . ."

"You aren't the only one with secrets and plans. Your mom gave me an assist. So did your friend Tasha."

"Tasha?"

"I ran into her on my way out the night you and your mother left me at your house. I waited around a couple of hours, but no more packages came and I had to get home. Tasha didn't even pretend to run into me accidentally. Said she saw me come over and was watching for me to leave so she could find out why I was hanging around your house, which she claims was her right to do as your best friend."

"Sounds like Tasha," I say. It makes me smile to know she still considers us best friends. I've been distracted and not holding up my end of that for a while.

"She had a few words for me. Something about dogging her friend."

"I'm gonna kill her."

"She was just looking out. I guess she filled you in on my extracurricular activity when I was at North DH."

"I'm really, *really* going to kill her."

"Don't, because it gives me a chance to clear that up. Most of those stories aren't true. Ask any quarterback—girls come with the position. Doesn't mean I take them up on their offers. But my friends . . . you know how guys are. It was easier to just go along with it."

"That time I saw you and Angelique at the TasteeTreets, I could tell y'all had history. And chemistry. I mean *serious* chemistry, and I've never even had a boyfriend. I figured that was another reason y'all hooked back up. She was more . . ."

"Angelique's great. You were right—my parents do love her. We've known each other since we were kids and we've been on and off again since ninth grade. But mostly we've been off. Outside of the 'serious chemistry,' there's not much else between us anymore. She was just, I don't know—"

"Comfortable?"

"Yeah, that's a good word for it. I figured it out that day you sat in your mom's car and we talked on the phone for an hour."

"But you had to hang up the call because you had a date with her."

"And the whole time I was with her, all I could think about was you. I ended it that night."

"You didn't tell me. . . ."

"Because I didn't think it mattered. There was still the problem with my parents, my cousin, your playing cop. But it wasn't fair to keep Angelique as my backup plan."

"Aren't your parents still a problem?" I ask.

"Probably, but they can't say it's because of David anymore. He decided to go back to Mexico."

"Oh no, not because your family's afraid I'm going to screw it up?"

"No, nothing like that. He just missed his parents."

"That's perfect, Marco. I mean, not for David, but—"

"David will be okay. And we still aren't totally in the clear. My parents still think you might get me killed, but eventually they'll see how great you are."

"I'm great?"

"Yes, and never, ever comfortable."

"What about the chemistry part?"

"You don't think we have chemistry? Because I know I'm feeling something right now."

"Um, you know what I mean. I noticed you said *most* of those player stories weren't true. I'm not ready for . . . I mean, don't guys think that's the important part?"

"It does rank pretty high, but there's a whole lot that happens between the first kiss and *serious* chemistry," he says. He smiles in that way that makes me think maybe I won't want to wait so long for the serious chemistry part to happen.

"Oh yeah? Like what?"

"Like riding a Vespa—"

"Yeah, riding that thing through Denver Heights will probably get you a beatdown. You know better than I do this ain't a scooter-riding kind of neighborhood."

"—to a sidewalk café where we'll sip champagne," Marco says, ignoring my interruption.

"I know it's a sunny day, but isn't it little chilly for that? And I'm turning sixteen, not twenty-one. I'm pretty sure we'll get carded if we try to order champagne."

"So we'll order ginger ale," Marco says, looking exasperated, at least until he smiles. "Will you stop playing detective for a second and let me finish telling you what comes between the first kiss and serious chemistry?"

I fold my arms across my chest and stay quiet.

"There's a ride in a horse-drawn carriage, buying gelato from a street vendor, and dancing—"

"Marco—you watched *Roman Holiday*," I squeal, and I *never* squeal.

"Today, we do whatever you want. I'm going to be the guy who helps you turn an ordinary sixteenth birthday into a fairy tale."

"You forgot one of the in-between things."

"Which one?"

"The kiss."

"Oh, I didn't forget that. But it doesn't happen until the end."

"I thought I get whatever I want."

"You're right," Marco says, putting his arms around my waist.

Finally, I'm going to get that second kiss I've been dying for since before we even broke up. I close my eyes and wait for it . . . and wait for it. . . .

"Sorry to interrupt, Chanti—but we need to talk."

That isn't Marco's voice. When I open my eyes to see who has just royally screwed up my moment, I find Cisco standing at the bottom of my porch steps. My sweet sixteen might not become a fairy tale after all, but considering the way my life's been going, it's definitely turning into an ordinary day.

GIRL DETECTIVE'S GLOSSARY

APB: *abbr.* All-points bulletin.

BOLO: *abbr.* Be on the lookout.

CI: *abbr.* Confidential informant. *slang.* snitch; narc.

CO: *abbr.* Commanding officer. A police officer's boss.

defendant: Person charged with a crime by the court.

Five-O: *slang.* 1. Police officer, detective, etc. 2. Black-and-white, po-po, the man.

MO: *abbr.* Modus operandi. How someone operates.

perp: *abbr.* Perpetrator. Person suspected of committing a crime.

plaintiff: Person charging a crime in the court.

prosecution: A court's case against a defendant.

running hot: Police car running with lights and sirens. Generally, patrol cars only run hot when something very bad is happening, like a crime in progress, and getting there fast is critical. If you reported your car broken into, they wouldn't run hot to your house to take your report. If someone was trying to break into your house, they would run hot.

street cop: Patrol officer, as opposed to a detective or ranking officer. 2. Beat cop, uniform.

vice unit: 1. Police department unit that usually handles narcotics, prostitution, and gambling crimes. 2. Where Chanti's mother Lana works undercover.

Meet Chanti for the first time in

My Own Worst Frenemy.

In stores now!

Turn the page for an excerpt of *My Own Worst Frenemy*. . . .

I'm eating Cocoa Puffs on my last day of summer vacation and watching the news because there's nothing else on but Sunday-morning church shows and infomercials. The reporter is on location, telling me how the police finally closed down a prostitution ring. I'd rather not share my breakfast with hookers or the helmet-haired reporter who's way too happy reporting their arrest, so I reach for the remote. That's when I recognize one of the women being loaded into the police truck. In case I'm not sure what I'm seeing, the reporter steps to the side and passes her arm through the air, Vanna White–style, so I can get a better look. The woman is trying to hide her face, and doing a good job, but I'd know that outfit anywhere.

It's definitely Lana, in her favorite wig, the platinum-blond one with the bangs. She's wearing a baby tee that reads YOUNG, WILLING, AND ABLE, with the neckline cut wide so one side slips off her shoulders to reveal a red bra strap. The T-shirt is cut so short that if not for the bra, all her business would be peeking out from the curled edges of cotton. If the shirt isn't bad enough, the Daisy Duke shorts are. And God, please don't let her bend over to duck into the truck like the other hookers are doing. Too late.

But that isn't the worst of it. People I know might be watching this. I might have to explain to them that my mother is not really a crack ho. Come to think of it, I'd be better off letting them think she *is* a crack ho since her real job is ten times worse. In my neighborhood, you can't get much lower than a vice cop.

A few hours later, no one has mentioned Lana or the fact that her butt cheeks were all over the news. It makes sense—none of my friends would be up that early on a Sunday, especially when it's our last day of freedom. We're spending it on my front porch doing what we've done pretty much all summer. Talking about being broke, gossiping about who hooked up and who broke up over the break, and trying to figure out what's going on at Ada Crawford's house across the street.

Ada's house doesn't fit in with the rest of the street. It was built in the fifties like the others, but her house is prettier, what real estate agents would call a *real cream puff* if anyone was actually interested in buying in our neighborhood. It's freshly painted and newly landscaped with the greenest grass that Ada has to water practically 24-7, which is no problem since she also has a new sprinkler system. Everybody else's house appears to have the original 1950s paint job, new landscaping is limited to plastic flowers on the porch, and we have to water our half-green, half-brown grass with a garden hose. What makes Ada a mystery is that she's got the nicest house on the block and no job. I know people can make a food stamp stretch, but not that much.

"It has something to do with all the men coming and going," I speculate. "There goes one now."

"Maybe she's a romantic and has lots of generous boyfriends, Chanti," Michelle offers.

"Riiight, she's a romantic. And please pronounce my name right—*Shawnty*, not *Shanty* like the towns where poor people live in a Steinbeck book."

"Who?" Michelle asks.

Maybe if she stopped calling me a book geek and picked one up herself, she'd find out. I know I sound a little testy, but Michelle annoys me. She's taken my best friend since third grade away from me, which is funny because Tasha and I never hung out with her before this summer. We even called her Squeak when she first moved on the block—not to her face or anything—because her voice reminded us of Minnie Mouse. Now they're almost besties. It isn't all Michelle's fault since I've been somewhat negligent in my best-friend duties and I suppose Tasha had to find someone to hang with all summer, but I'm still a little peeved.

"Well, she can't be dealing, because someone else has cornered that market, right, Michelle?" Tasha says as she glues a track onto Michelle's scalp. Tasha's mom can't stand the smell of the glue, so she has to do all her weaving outside. Most people would be afraid to get their weave done on somebody's porch by a girl with no professional training, but Tasha is a lot cheaper than the salon and really has a way with hair. She's like the weave whisperer or something.

There's a loud bang and Michelle jumps out of her chair and ducks behind the glider swing, ripping the newly glued track right off her head because Tasha is still holding it.

"What is your problem?" Tasha asks.

"I thought I heard a gunshot."

"I know this isn't the farm, but it's not *that* bad, Michelle," I say. "Mr. Harrison is trying to get his lawnmower started. It always sounds like that."

Michelle comes out from behind the glider and returns to her chair. "Now it's my turn to correct you—I lived on a ranch, not a farm."

"Close enough," I say.

"Michelle isn't too far off the mark," Tasha defends her. "Isn't that why you aren't working at Tastee Treets anymore?"

"My mother made me quit because a meth-head held us up, even though I was in the back walk-in freezer sneaking some Rocky Road during the whole thing," I say. "Besides, that guy pulled a gun—he didn't shoot it."

"Well, I heard somebody did get shot last weekend, a couple blocks over," Tasha says.

Tasha knows everything about our neighborhood, but I know there wasn't a shooting two blocks over because Lana would have been talking about it for days. It would have been another justification for making me change schools, which she decided to do when my school announced it was closing. After years of people leaving for the suburbs, our school was down to five hundred students so the city merged it into our rival, North High. Lana won't move because she says if we wait a minute, it won't be long before someone opens an Asian bistro, a yoga studio, and a Starbucks on Center Street and we'll be all gentrified, like what happened in some other Denver neighborhoods. Then she plans to sell for a lot of money. Lana is more optimistic than I am. I think we'll be waiting longer than a minute for that to happen.

"Chanti, you can't convince your mother to let you go with us to North?" Tasha says. She knows me so well, it's like she can read my mind. I bet she can't do that with Squeak.

"It's the day before school starts. What do *you* think?"

I've been telling her all summer that nothing I say will make Lana change her mind about forcing me to go to some stuck-up rich school across town just because I made one little mistake. She thinks I'll get into more trouble if I stay in Denver Heights and go to North.

"Don't get attitudinal on me, Chanti. I'm not the one who screwed up my life."

I ignore Tasha and do the only thing I can given the situation: I lie.

"The only thing worse than going to a school you hate is starting a new school after everyone else. Even if Lana lets me go to North, by the time the transfer paperwork happened, I'd be starting three weeks late. By then, everyone will have staked out their tables in the cafeteria. All the back seats in class will be taken. I'd rather go to the new school on day one than start North late and be the new girl."

"That would be tragic," says Michelle in the only tone she seems to know—sarcastic. "Ow, Tasha. Stop pulling!"

"At least I didn't choose my school based on a boy," I say to Michelle, who gives me the finger. "A boy so sorry he gets kicked out of school before he even started it, and in the meantime spends the summer cheating on me with Rhonda Hodges so I have to break up with him anyway."

Michelle looks sincerely wounded now, not just from the way Tasha is handling her head, and I feel bad for adding on that last part. But not as bad as I feel about her messing up me and Tasha's perfectly good friendship. Although I'm sure Tasha would say I was the one who messed things up.

"You wouldn't be new," Tasha says. "You'd know me and Michelle, and a bunch of other people from the old school. Not to mention kids from around the way, like . . ."

"Speaking of kids from The Ave," I say, cutting her off because there's no chance of me going to North and it bums me out talking about it. "Did y'all hear about Donnell Down-the-Street?"

"What about him?"

"He got picked up." I say this as though it's old news, knowing that neither of them have heard a thing about Donnell Down-the-Street. We call him that because there are two Donnells on Aurora Avenue, where I live. The one closest to Center Street got to keep his name without anything added on. The other one got arrested yesterday. I only know this because Lana told me during this morning's tirade entitled *Chanti, You're Going to That School and Donnell Is Just Another Example Why—As If We Need More Examples—and You Better Not Ask Me Again Because You're Going and That's All There Is to It.*

"No he didn't!" Michelle says without a hint of sarcasm. Until recently (well, until Rhonda Hodges), she had a serious thing for Donnell DTS. "For what? How do you know?"

"I just do."

Tasha vouches for me. "Chanti always knows this stuff before everyone else. She just does."

My friends can never know Lana is my source. They think she's a paralegal in an office downtown. That's because when you're Vice and all the undercover cases you work are related to drugs, prostitution, or gambling, it's all about the down low. The minute anyone figures out she's a cop, she'll have to leave Vice and go back to the burglary division, which she says is nowhere near as exciting. Lana guards her secret like Michelle guards the fact she is no longer a virgin (thanks to Donnell DTS) from her preacher daddy. But I know all about Michelle because Tasha can't keep her mouth shut. I keep it to myself because that's one of the things I do well, hold on to other people's business. You never know when you might need it.

Information is negotiable, like currency. I learned that from Lana. Not information like her identity, of course. That secret keeps us both safe. It's the reason I call her Lana instead of Mom, even though everyone knows her by a totally different name on the street. Thanks to great genes and the fact that she had me when she was just sixteen, Lana looks too young to be my mother, which is kind of helpful. The fewer people who know I'm her kid, the better. Some of her more vindictive perps would be happy to know she has a kid. Except for my grandparents in Atlanta, I'm the only one outside the department who knows what she really does—we don't have family in town and Lana's closest friends are cops. So keeping Lana's secret sort of makes me her partner. It's like I'm kind of a cop, and it doesn't matter that I'm way too scared to actually ever *be* a cop.

Just as I'm about to tell them what I know—which is

nothing, but I'm very good at embellishing—we see MJ Cooper walking toward us, on the other side of the street. Tasha and Michelle go quiet because they're too busy trying to watch MJ without actually looking at her. Well, I'm not afraid to look at her, and I do. That's why I notice that she stops for just a second, like she might consider crossing the street, but she gives me a look that almost strikes me down where I'm standing, then keeps walking.

Michelle speaks first, but only when she's certain MJ is halfway down the block. "What's *she* looking at?"

"Seems like she's still mad at you, Chanti," Tasha says. "What did you do to her, anyway? Whatever it was, I think you best watch your back."

"Please. She's just been watching too many reruns of *The Wire*. Thinks she's Snoop Pearson or somebody," Michelle says. "Nobody's scared of her."

"Chanti's mother is. That's why she's sending her away to school."

Tasha thinks she knows everything.

"It isn't *away*. It's like ten miles from here, and I'll be taking the bus there and back every day."

"Well, MJ's still the reason," Tasha says, smug in being right.

"I wonder if she had anything to do with the police harassing Donnell," Michelle says.

My natural instinct is about to kick in, the one that makes me angry whenever anyone acts like the cops are the bad guys, but I let it go. Because around here, where profiling was probably invented, sometimes they *are* the bad guys. Still, if anyone on The Ave is prime for getting picked up, it's Donnell DTS, if not for whatever he did last night, then surely for something else.

"Donnell doesn't need to be harassed," I remind Michelle. "It isn't his fault he's like that."

"Whose fault is it?" Tasha asks.

"My daddy says it's because he doesn't have a father fig-ure. He sees that a lot in his congregation."

"You mean his church of twenty that he holds in your basement?" Tasha asks.

"It'll be a big church one day and you won't be talking smack then," Michelle says. "He used to have a good-size congregation when we lived in Texas."

"My father skipped out before I was born and you don't see me going to jail," I say. "It's Donnell's third time in. Don't make like he's a choirboy."

"It's only his second time," Michelle says, as if it still makes him eligible for that choirboy job. "Not that I'm de-fending him or anything."

"Yeah, you are, and you need to give it up," Tasha adds. "Donnell ain't thinking about you, especially if he's in jail. If he's thinking about anything other than how his public de-fender is going to get him off, it's going to be how he can get even with Chanti."

Uh, what?

"Why does he care anything about her?" Michelle asks, looking at me suspiciously.

"I heard he knows it was Chanti who told you about Rhonda Hodges."

"How would he know that unless you told?" I ask Michelle.

"Because I told," she says, seeming not to care one bit that I now have an ex-con gunning for me. That'll be the last time I mind someone else's business.

"I also heard MJ isn't talking to Chanti because she double-crossed her."

"Tasha, how come half your sentences start with 'I heard'?" I say, angry not so much with Tasha's gossiping than with the fact that she's probably right on both counts.

"You used to ask me for the scoop all the time, Chanti. Now that it's about you, suddenly you don't want to hear it."

Tasha doesn't understand. I'm starting eleventh grade and never had a real boyfriend, I have to keep my mother's job a secret on a block where the truth would get us run out at gunpoint, and I have to start a new school tomorrow. With all that going on, I really don't need to hear two crazy ex-cons might have it in for me.